A Good Life

Sarah Rowan

To Davi,
Thanks for supporting
M

Amazing Things Press

Book design by Julie L. Casey

This book is a work of fiction. Any names, characters, or incidents are the product of the author's imagination and are used fictitiously. Any resemblance to actual events, locales, or persons, living or dead is purely coincidental.

ISBN 978-1945667039

Printed in the United States of America.

For more information, visit
www.amazingthingspress.com

This book is dedicated to everyone suffering from an undiagnosed mental illness.

Dear Susan,

I hope you find this letter easily. I tried to hide it in a place that only you would be able to find. You would think that this would be painful to write, but I've never been happier. I know, I know that you are hurting. It is hard to lose someone you love. Believe me, I would know.

I'm finally free now. Free from the horror of life, from the night terrors, the obligations.

After they go through my things, I want you to pry up the floorboards under my bed. I've left something for you that my family cannot know about. Something that would make your life better. You were the only one that I could ever trust. You, with your sweet smile and cocky ways. You are just like Livi. I just wish you would let yourself be your authentic self.

Tell Sam I love her.

Tell Allison to stay free.

Tell Adia to fuck off.

I know that you're thinking that I'm an idiot for doing this. Well, I just can't keep holding everyone back. This is my gift to the world and the world's gift to me. I'm finally taking back what the world took from me. To live, I must die.

I love you,
Ted.

One

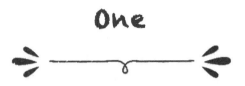

Emerson never died.

A house stood there in the middle of the lawn. The surrounding grass was up to Susan's knees and a tire leaned up against the porch railing. Susan smiled. The delightful, pale blue paint was peeling and the cement sidewalk was cracked. Perfect. It was the kind of dilapidated beauty that you find in country songs. It had one lonely maple tree in the corner of the yard, providing ample shade to the garden snake resting near the trunk. A white, wooden fence separated it from the surrounding downtown shacks and broken down cars.

She placed her hands on her hips and stood in the driveway, surveying the neighborhood. There were several rundown houses with boarded up windows, but here and there, well-kept ancient houses stood out like lone flowers growing among weeds. The neighborhood was an old man, distinguished, but in fading health surrounded by his grandchildren, vibrant and cosmopolitan. It was located just south of downtown Omaha in what was known as "Little Italy." In its heyday, it was a bustling center of prohibition bootlegging and Sicilian restaurants. Now it was filled with impoverished and abandoned buildings. Homeless people carrying brown bags occupied the occasional nook of an alleyway and Susan took note of a couple of supposed drug deals in progress.

"It's not much, Susie, but I like how close it is to The Old Market." A man opened the trunk of the car. He was tall with a lanky physique. His reddish brown beard added a contrast to the early summer warmth, but accentuated his angular face.

"Oh, c'mon, Ted." Susan flung her hands in the air and turned to face him. "'Never lose an opportunity of seeing anything beautiful, for beauty is God's handwriting.' There is plenty of that here! It's art, in its own way. A slightly unkempt property shows honesty. Honesty is beautiful!" She picked up one of her cardboard boxes and made her way to the house, stepping over sticks and the occasional rock.

"Way to put your degree to use!" Ted laughed.

"I dwell in pretension, my dear boy." She twisted the brass doorknob and kicked the door open, keeping her balance. Exhaling, she set the box down on the wooden floor. "Damn, that was heavy."

3

"I could've carried it for you," Ted offered as he set down some of his own stuff down alongside hers.

Susan scowled.

"Oh, I'm sorry," he chuckled. "I forgot that you were still on that angry, militant, feminist kick."

"It's not a kick. I was just tired of Ben's chauvinism and mistreatment of me." She stretched her back. "Chauvinism is *such* a turn-off. Male or female."

"Are you sure you're not a lesbian?" Ted grinned.

Susan punched him in the shoulder. "Anyway, I'm glad you found this place." She approached the wooden staircase and noted the dark varnish on the steps. "It has plenty of character."

"I agree." Ted took off his stocking cap and wiped his forehead. "It was once my great aunt's place before The Great War. We've been kinda keeping it up since she died a few years ago, but you really can't tell from the outside." He placed his cap back on his head.

"Awesome opossum." She felt the grain of the banister. "It has history." She looked him in the face. "I'm very grateful that your parents are leasing it out to us...and for only $800 a month!"

"Yeah, it's a steal," he smiled. *"Everyone*

wants to live in a neighborhood full of crack-heads!"

"It's a beautiful house, Ted." She inhaled. "Should I pick up some mace?"

"Naw, I don't think so. You'll be fine. You're pretty kick-ass."

Susan went back to the car for her second load.

Ted followed. "If we have time later, we should go find some furniture."

"Is there a thrift store around here?"

Ted shrugged, "I don't remember. But hey, we could do our furniture shopping like we did in college."

Susan paused, her blond hair falling across her face. She pushed it back behind her ear. "You know, I really don't feel like scavenging about for thrown out furniture."

"Yeah... You're right. We don't want surprise rats like last time." He picked up a suitcase. "'When we were in college.' It makes me feel old."

"We just graduated *yesterday*, hon."

"Heheh."

"C'mon. I don't want to spend all day doing this. I'd like to relax at some point." She gave thanks that she was a natural athlete. It made her job so much easier on her slender frame. The black tank top and jeans accentuated her toned muscles as she removed yet another cardboard box from her car. She rushed back into the house.

"Okay, okay. I won't slack off anymore." He put his hands in the air and resumed the repetitive practice of unloading the car.

Thanks to their moving sale and college life, they had very little to move and the process of running back and forth to the car took only thirty minutes. Soon they were sitting in the center of the floor amid boxes and sipping on pop.

Ted lit a cigarette. "I'm so glad that's over."

"I feel ya." She lay on her back. "I hate moving." She sat back up and took another drink. "Think we'll find jobs?"

"Yeah, Omaha has a low unemployment rate." He took a puff. "Although with your English degree, you'd be lucky to work fast food." He grinned.

Susan threw the now empty pop bottle at him. "Shut the fuck up, dude. Like your degree is any better."

He rolled his eyes. "Yeah, *no one* wants to hire an accountant. Anyway, you shouldn't have a problem finding a job. You're smart, kinda attractive, and have had good luck in the past."

"Yeah…"

Fear gripped her. She hid it away before Ted could notice. *I'm probably going to fall into the percentage of Americans underemployed or employed in a profession unrelated to their field. I don't want to be a peon or a manager at the local McDonald's. Can't I find happiness? I know, without a doubt, that I probably will commit suicide within the first five years of graduation. Ted does not need to know this. He has no reason to, his life is carefree and predictable. Within those five years, he will probably marry, and have a couple of kids. He will never find this out, until after I die. Even then, it's doubtful.* Despite their close friendship, almost bordering on romantic, she still kept most of her secrets away from him. She sighed.

Ted unpacked his copy of *The Over-Soul and Other Essays* by Ralph Waldo Emerson and blankly flipped through it. "We shall start job hunting tomorrow. For now, let's get food."

"Agreed." She grabbed her purse and they left to find the nearest Pizza Run.

Two

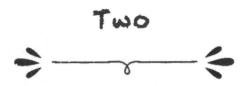

Ted woke to rays of sunlight invading his eyelids. He winced. *Sometimes mornings are great, this one, not so much.* Fishing for his cell phone, he knocked off a stack of paperback books from the nightstand. Old compendiums of comic books went tumbling down as he continued to flail about.

"Ugnugugnn." He finally yanked his phone off the wall charger. It sparked a little. Ted gave it a blank stare and rubbed his eyes. He checked the time. 9:00 AM. *Is this for real? I could have sworn that I set it for eight.* Needing more sleep but realizing that it would be futile to fight the sunlight, he slowly rolled himself off of his mattress and onto the cold wooden floor. Lying on his stomach, he searched for a somewhat presentable pair of jeans and a t-shirt.

He lifted himself and scratched his beard. *Should I shave?* He glanced into the mirror and shook his head. Ted rubbed his eyes and grabbed a nearby bottle of whiskey and took a couple of swigs. He checked his phone again. 9:10. *Mom wouldn't care if I were late. She should have learned to expect this from me a long time ago.* He scavenged for a blazer in the closet and picked up a strewn red stocking cap. *The occasion calls for it, after all.* He took another swig and tied his low-top sneakers.

He sauntered down the hall to make some eggs. *Man, I want those eggs. Eggs with cheddar. Maybe I should throw in some hot salsa?* Whistling, he noticed that Susan was not up and about yet, so he resolved to be as quiet as possible. The eggs hissed in the frying pan. He started a pot of coffee. *Wait, whiskey would be better.* He picked up a bottle of Jack Daniels and glanced at the coffee. *Susan will drink it.*

"Damn you, eggs. Be quiet." He slid them onto a paper plate and scarfed them down with a whiskey chaser.

Leaving the pan in the sink with a slight clang, he left the house, returned for his phone, and left again. This time, he succeeded in unlocking the car and leaving the driveway. With folk music blaring, he was ready to tackle the thirty-minute drive to West Omaha.

He drove through the gate to the brick house surrounded by trimmed hedges and gardenias. The scent of them sickened Ted. He hid his vomit behind the bushes and under some mulch. Wiping his mouth with his handkerchief, he popped a breath mint and rang the doorbell. His brother answered.

"About fucking time you showed up." His displeasure accentuated by the black business suit and manicured goatee.

Typical Chuck.

"Meh. Traffic was a bitch."

Rolled eyes and a sigh welcomed him into the house. Ted made his way to the living room, strolling past paintings of Nebraskan farms and family portraits. He groaned in disgust as he passed the scenes of cows and barns. *So many barns.*

"Happy graduation, Ted!" His mother trapped him in her monstrous arms.

"Thanks."

She gave him a once over. "Why aren't you wearing a suit?"

"I am." He tugged on his blazer.

She tightened her lips and shook her head. "That doesn't count, Teddy."

He shrugged. "I tried."

"You should pay more attention to how you present yourself." She tugged on his beard. "You'll never be taken seriously in the business world with this scruff." She let go. "Come on, now. We've been waiting. You need to work on your punctuality."

Ted stared ahead as they continued.

They entered the rather large dining room

and seated themselves around a long wooden table amid summery floral arrangements and more Nebraskan landscapes. They were joined by Ted's father, Chuck, an uncle and aunt with a couple female cousins, and his grandparents. Amid the business suits and summer dresses, was a brunch layout fit for twice as many people. There were omelets, hash browns, fruit, and lots and lots of waffles. Typical greasy Nebraskan fare. The Spencer's loved large meals, but somehow (with the exception of some of the women) managed to maintain good figures. Ted thought he spied some Greek yogurt in the corner. He was handed some coffee by his adjacent cousin. He chugged it. There was some muffled disapproval of his tardiness as he settled himself into his chair.

His father poured him some more coffee.

Ted said nothing.

On his opposite side, his mother nudged him.

"Uh, thanks, dad."

"You're welcome, Teddy!" He smiled. "I know how hard it is for a young man to wake up in the morning," he winked and lowered his voice, "especially living with such a fox!"

Ted lowered his eyes and sipped his coffee.

His mother cleared her throat. "We are so proud of our oldest son graduating college!" She shook him. "He's going to go far in life!" Her face beamed.

Chuck sat across from Ted and poured some cream into his coffee. "Do you have a job yet?"

Ted shifted in his seat. "Uhh…no. I've put some applications in with a few corporations, but I've only had one interview so far and not many callbacks. But Dad said he'd also interview me."

Chuck smirked. "Well, let's hope they like unkempt 'dudes.'"

"Chuck, be nice." said Mrs. Spencer.

Ted coughed, "Douchebag."

"Don't worry, Ted." His dad winked and smiled. "I've already hired you."

Mrs. Spencer didn't notice Ted's comeback as she placed her napkin on her lap.

Mr. Spencer cleared his throat and stood up. "Sibling squabbles aside, we are here to congratulate Theodore Joseph Spencer III on obtaining a Bachelor's of Science in Accounting!" He lifted his cup into the air. "Cheers!"

The table applauded.

"Too bad Olivia isn't here to see it," Chuck muttered as the applause died down. His mother shot him a stern look.

Mr. Spencer sat down. "Now, let's eat!"

Ted sneaked some whiskey into his coffee. He shifted in his seat and occupied his time with idle chatter until brunch was over. Afterward, he planned to disappear into his old bedroom for a while to sort through some old things to take to the new house. There were also some paintings that his mother decided did not "fit" with the current décor of the family's home that he wanted to sift through. *Maybe find some of my old high school artwork. Hopefully, it isn't destroyed.*

Three

Susan scoured the classified ads in the newspaper for job postings. She found a plethora of openings for cashiers, accountants, etc., but only a handful for anything related to English. Of those ads, only experienced people were wanted. *How the hell can you get experience without an opportunity for experience?* A sigh escaped her lips as she sipped her coffee.

Her mouth was taken hostage by the distinct taste of burnt coffee.

"Dammit, Ted, can't you fix a cup of coffee!" Her frustration was directed toward Ted's first floor bedroom although she knew he wasn't home.

She slid the paper across the table and checked her phone. 10:00 am. No messages. Disappointment rippled through her veins. Of course Ben hadn't messaged her. Of course none of her friends had messaged her either. They were living it up back in Missouri while she was stuck in Omaha, jobless and, aside from Ted, alone.

Susan paced the kitchen from the table to the

coffeemaker and back again. She yearned for something she couldn't describe. She paced again, glanced outside, and noticed a gentle rain shower. Another pace. Another glance.

"Maybe I will go outside and take a walk," she muttered to herself. She *did* need to replace her coffee anyway. Looking back at the newspaper with a slight sense of guilt, she decided to pick up a couple of applications while she was out. Might as well be productive while slacking off. She went to change.

Wearing dark skinny jeans with a long red t-shirt, flats, and a beret, she grabbed her umbrella and headed out the door. She looked a million bucks, but felt half a grand. It took five attempts to lock the wooden door. She was still used to the old apartment. Cursing, she secured the door and descended the porch steps.

Despite her bad mood, the rain was beautiful and Susan felt a tinge of warmth in her chest. Coupled with the acoustic rock on her mp3 player, it soothed some of her pain. She soon found herself smiling as she meandered down wet streets among gray buildings. The rain made the buildings sheen with a romance found only in movies about New York City and down-on-their-luck hipsters. She lost herself in this real life film and soon forgot why she had ventured out of the house.

Coffee.

She needed coffee.

There *had* to be a coffee shop *somewhere* around here. Susan traveled further than she intended and had somehow, in her reverie, ended up in a neighborhood just a few blocks south of The Old Market and north of Little Italy.

She walked around the block and then realized that there was a coffee shop right where she had started her circle. A brick façade stood out among the limestone businesses with a couple of large windowpanes adorned with a steaming coffee cup and beans. The words "Cool Beans" were painted above the cup in blue and purple paint. *There's no one here, but I need my caffeine fix. I don't care if it has a great chance of being crappy.*

The flood of coffee aroma with touches of patchouli incense enticed her as she entered the quaint shop. It was a medium sized shop with several armchairs scattered among standard wooden chairs. There was a stage area by the front window and a bare bulletin board to the left of it. The plain counter was in an alcove at the far end of the shop with a menu overhead. She read through the offerings and decided on a simple caramel cappuccino.

It was then that she discovered that there wasn't a clerk behind the counter. She looked around to no avail until she finally noticed a bell. She rang for service.

A shortish man with long, blond dreads came out from a stockroom. He had a standard black apron on over a plaid shirt and jeans with several tattoos and facial piercings. The smell of weed almost overwhelmed her senses.

"'Sup." He widened his eyes. "How may I help you?"

"Uh...I'd like a small caramel cappuccino, please."

"Righteous. Two bucks, please." He took his time making her drink.

She handed him her card. "Thank you."

"No, thank you, dear madam. Here's your card back." He smiled and went back to the stock room.

Susan's brow furrowed as she watched him disappear. *Should I be concerned?* The thought was dismissed as she as she took her first sip.

It was Nirvana.

She smiled and left the shop.

Susan stood under the canopy outside the coffee shop. She sipped on her coffee as the cold rain formed a puddle by the fire hydrant. The cappuccino's foam tickled her lip. Its caramel flavor added an elegance to her late morning walk. She paused for a moment on a lone, dry bench by the door. Its green paint was peeling, revealing old pine. People rushed down the street in suits and skirts on their way to work, speaking on cell phones and drinking lattes from the Starbucks around the corner. She took another sip, savoring the creamy taste. She closed her eyes, enjoying the environment and sending a little positivity to the world. *Finally, I am able to relax for the first time in a week.*

She opened her eyes to the same scene, but prayed that the passersby would learn to slow down. A raindrop splashed into a puddle, causing a ripple to form and dissipate. She meditated upon this for a moment. *Such simplicity amid such complexity.* Her foot tapped to the beat of the music in her ear and the scene drifted out of focus.

An umbrella closing caught her attention and she turned to her left. A brunette with long hair and brown faux-leather boots was stomping her feet on the welcome mat outside the door. Above her, a neon green paper sign read "NOW HIRING. APPLY INSIDE." Susan looked at her coffee. *How could I have missed that sign? Was it not there five minutes ago?* She looked at her coffee again, considering the situation. *Should I really apply here? Would it pay my bills?* She weighed her options for a few moments and ventured back into the coffee shop.

The guy with the dreads pointed at her, lifted

his head, grinned and said, "Welcome back, yo. Heh heh."

The brunette shook her head as she wiped some mugs. "Chris, stop harassing the customers."

Chris just grinned and stared at Susan, "Want more coffee?"

"Uh...no..." Susan looked at her nearly empty cup.

"On the house."

"Sure."

"Righteous." He bobbed his head and took the cup away from her.

"Thanks. I'd also like an application, please." She tucked a wayward strand of hair behind her ear.

The brunette turned around at the mention of an application, still polishing a mug. She looked at Susan's feet and let her gaze wander to her face and back again.

"Here ya go," Chris handed her a napkin with a web address scrawled on it along with her refill. "We like to save our mother Earth."

"Thank you." Susan looked at it and sipped on her coffee as she left the store.

"Hire her," she overheard the brunette say to Chris in an audible whisper.

Four

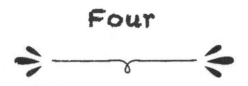

"It really is quite jarring, isn't it?" Allison poured her brother some coffee. She inhaled the aroma. *Strong and pungent. Appropriate for a dark Sumatra roast fresh from the bag.* She handed the light blue cup over to Chris who sat across the coffee table.

He sipped the coffee and closed his eyes. "Yeah, it would be totally awesome in the morning."

"Especially on days when you don't want to leave your bed." Allison gestured with her finger.

"I want to start selling this."

"I think that would be a great idea." She surveyed the shop. Save for themselves, it was vacant.

Allison poured herself a cup. Hers was pink with a little white kitten on it. *Cute, but I hate it. That's why it's in the shop and not my personal collection.* She sipped and savored the bold coffee without cream or sugar. Setting it down on the table, she watched as the ripples bounced back and forth against the edge. She sat there for a moment and took out her sketchpad and pencils.

It was true that the shop gave her much needed inspiration. It had abstract art on the walls in various shades of red. *Red is awesome. It has so many shades, each bold and vibrant in its own way. Red draws your attention to the work and overshadows any flaws. A work with flaws is not perfect, but it is genuine.* Allison channeled her art professor. *Sometimes the artist intends such flaws, allowing the viewer to draw out a much more thorough interpretation of the work. Red is the perfect color for this purpose.*

Red is bold and vibrant, just like this coffee. She sipped and stared at the paintings on the wall. Not one of them had been sold, thanks to the lack of patronage. Allison decided to sketch out a commemorative portrait of sorts of the shop, first in pencil and then overlaid with red watercolors. She sat there in that plush armchair, drawing soft lines here and hard lines there for an hour before calling it quits. She was at work after all. She stowed her sketchpad and supplies away in her messenger bag and set it on the table. There was no one there to steal it anyway. Her stomach growled. "Chris, I'm going to lunch."

"Okay."

She grabbed her purse and left the store. *I'm*

really feeling a sandwich today. She bumped shoulders with some man and mumbled an apology as she turned the corner to the mom and pop sandwich shop next door.

When she returned, she set her umbrella by the door and saw Chris sneak into the storage closet. *He's probably smoking.* She shook her head and started dusting some cups. Allison sighed. *These cups are pathetic.* Most of them had never been used in the month that Cool Beans had been open. Still, she dusted and washed them once a day, kicking herself because it was a waste of water and money.

"Merrr..." she groaned.

Clink. Clink. Clink.

She soon fell into a trance.

Clink. Clink. Clink.

She was one with the cups.

The door chimed. It escaped her ears.

Pull cup out.

Wipe cup.

Put cup back.

Clink. Clink. Clink.

Her back was to the counter so she did not see the young blonde woman approaching. She heard Chris's soft but masculine voice greet someone. "Chris, stop harassing the customers." Finishing the last cup, she turned around.

Standing before her was an exquisite example of feminine beauty. The woman was perfectly proportioned with an aura of masculinity. *Girlish clothes.* Allison's eyes wandered from the floor upward. *Boyish stature.* She met her face. *Blue eyes like none other.*

She watched their exchange before the woman's eventual hypnotic, exit from the store.

"Hire her," she said impulsively to Chris.

He smiled and gave a double thumbs up, "That would be righteous." His eyes still glazed, "But can we afford another person?"

Allison rolled her eyes, "She'd probably draw in more male customers."

Chris squinted his eyes. "I see that your lesbian sense is tingling." He made jazz hands in the air.

"Eff you." She rolled her eyes again as he returned to the storage room.

Five

Ted stared at the ceiling tiles until they faded and melded together. Just twelve years before, this was her room. You could still see the letters O.S. Carved into the wooden baseboards, but the pink wallpaper was replaced by a more masculine blue. The ceiling had been deep cleaned and painted over. There was no trace of blood spatter left. *Why the fuck am I staying the night? Jesus Christ, I'm an idiot.*

He closed his eyes.

So much screaming.
So much blood.

Ted awoke thrashing the covers. Sweat dripped down his face and he couldn't breathe. He put on his glasses and looked out the window. Leaves waved back at him. *Just a dream. Just a motherfucking dream. It's not my fault.* Lying to himself soothed his rapid heart. He got up and slid on his shoes. *Beer.* He checked the time. 3:30. *Too late to purchase alcohol.*

He pulled on a loose hoodie and left the front

door unlocked. There happened to be a twenty-four hour convenience store just six blocks away. If he walked, he could leave and return unnoticed.

Ted opened the door to the fresh scent of nighttime rain. The streetlights illuminated the sidewalk in silver. His headphones muffled his footsteps as he passed by trees and high value homes.

The door chimed as he entered and he gave a passing "hello" to the man at the counter. He sauntered around the aisles half looking at snacks and pop until the cashier turned around. At the first opportunity, he slid a cool 24 ounce can under his jacket. *Not enough to get me drunk, but enough to calm my nerves*. He approached the counter. *I must buy something.*

"How may I help you?" the cashier droned.

Ted glanced at the cigarettes behind the counter. "Marlboro Reds and a lighter." That was the first thing that popped into his head and his first pack of cigarettes.

"ID." The cashier took his license, glanced at it, and handed it back to him. "$6.16."

Ted slid his card into his pocket, took the cigarettes with the lighter, and left.

He waited until he turned the corner before snapping the can open. *Thank God the cops don't come around here often*. He chugged it and lit a cigarette. He puffed a few times and watched the smoke curl and twist. *Not bad.* He grinned to himself and let out a little cough.

Opening his house door, he slid into his room and fell upon the bed. The night terrors didn't plague him the rest of the night.

He had an epiphany after his morning oatmeal. *I should celebrate my new job and throw a huge blowout at the new house. Maybe this will help me feel more at home.* Ted felt a tinge of sadness in his chest. *I miss that about college. The carefree parties, the laughter, the happiness. Omaha has remained the same as it was before I left. It's oppressing, depressing, and possessing of very few carefree memories. I need this party.*

His hand shook as he put the spoon to his mouth. Olivia was there beside him, eating. Her blonde hair dangling in a ponytail, her smile sweet as sugar as she told him about the exciting track meet that weekend and the following sleepover.

"It's going to be so awesome, Teddy!" she squealed.

"I don't want another girl in the house. They're weird and annoying."

She giggled. "Oh, Teddy, you're just eleven. You don't know *anything* yet."

"Teddy, Teddy." Someone snapped their fingers in his eyes. Mrs. Spencer was there, sipping on coffee. "Teddy, I said you don't know anything yet, so you shouldn't assume your brother's girlfriend is weird and annoying."

"Ok." He munched his oats and sipped on his orange juice. *What was that? I could have sworn Livi was there. Are the nightmares turning into daydreams?* He dismissed the thought. *It's probably because I didn't sleep well.* "I think I will throw a party, Mom, to celebrate my new job. Charlie's girlfriend can come too. In fact, I'm going to invite all my Omaha friends." He drank some juice. "Well, the ones I have on Facebook." He feigned a chuckle.

"You kids and your Facebooks." She shook her head as she placed her cup in the sink. "In my day, we talked *in person*, not over the Internet."

Six

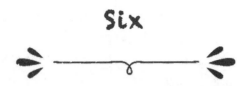

"Mothereffer." Allison flung her umbrella in the closet, spraying water all over her shoe collection. "Ugh!" She opened her drenched bag and took out her sodden sketchpad. "Stupid mothereffing wind." She flipped through the pages, crying, and tossed it across the room, missing her cat.

She kicked her milk crate ottoman. "Eff my life! What a waste of twenty dollars!" She threw her fists into the air and winced. Opening her eyes and walking to the window overlooking a rain soaked alley, she scowled. Each raindrop was a needle pricking her irritation. She yanked the curtains shut and grabbed her lighter. *Incense.*

She placed a stick of patchouli in each of her incense burners scattered throughout her studio apartment and she lit them one by one. Smoke soon enveloped both her and her cat as she inhaled. She sat lotus style in the center of a handwoven rug and breathed in deeply. *I must find my center. I need peace.* In and out she breathed. Allison felt the frustration exiting through her pores. Emptiness replaced it. Emptiness was calmness. Calmness was peace.

Thirty minutes passed before she was able to focus herself once again on the here and now. She exhaled and opened her eyes. She rediscovered the center of her being.

She glanced at the sketchpad lying in the corner. It would have to be replaced, but something stirred her soul. *Do I really need to confine myself to the conventional paper medium? Should I not experiment in something untested?* She picked up her orange tabby and cradled him in her arms. Her brow furrowed as she stood. Inspiration delivered goosebumps.

Her lips formed the words as they echoed through the apartment. "Street art."

How would I go about it? The cat purred as she paced her apartment. *What message would I deliver? What materials would I use? Would this make me a ninja?*

Allison sat and pondered the logistics. *Spray paint would probably be the ideal medium. As for the canvas, I would have to explore Omaha a bit more. I need some place easily visible, but not too visible. I don't want to make prison my new home.*

"Hmm...Mr. Scruffles, what do you think?" She looked down at the cat.

"Merrow." Mr. Scruffles closed his eyes.

"Of course, you can't read my mind." She smiled.

She felt two vibrations in her pocket as her phone received a text message from Chris.

Come to this kick ass house party, yo.

The vintage clock chimed nine times. *What type of party would be awesome at nine?*

"Oh right, everything's awesome when you're stoned," she sighed to the cat.

Checking her calendar, she discovered that she did not have to be at work in the morning. *Might as well go out. Beats staying at home.*

What's the address?

Her thumb swiped the screen. She hopped into the shower.

Allison donned a cute floral dress with red flowers and puffed sleeves. She slid on black thigh high slouched socks and red Mary Janes. Stretching a black belt just under her bust, she decided a beret would best keep the frizz away. Her lipstick matched her shoes when she finished her makeup. Soon after, she got in her car, spritzed some perfume, and sped away.

Parking a half block away because of the number of cars alongside the road, she clutched her mace as she approached the door. She didn't have to open it as the screen was left swinging in the breeze. She crept inside, trying not to be awkward. Upon entering, she couldn't move, let alone breathe, because of the crowd.

Where the eff is Chris? She looked back and forth and then took out her phone to text her brother. There was no need as she heard her name shouted above the dubstep.

"Allie! Wazzup!" Chris held his beer high as he parted the crowd, wearing a big, goofy grin on his face. He did some sort of jig as he forced a beer into his sister's hand. "Drink, lil' sis! And mingle! You might get laid!"

Allison opened her mouth to respond, but he cut her off.

"I saw a few gay lookin' girls in the back. They were makin' out, yo!" Chris stumbled over to chat with a red bearded hipster.

She rolled her eyes. *This is why I don't party with him very much.* Allison scanned the crowd for a familiar face. *No one. Great.* She sighed and thought back to her intro to theatre class.

Fake that you're outgoing, and you will be outgoing, she remembered her professor saying. Allison gulped and opened her beer.

That's when she saw her. The blonde from earlier. She was standing to the side of a bunch of pretty boy jock types. Allison sipped from her beer and gagged. *Nasty cheap beer.* She wiped her lips. *Maybe I should talk to her?* She forced another sip and inched closer to the girl.

"Whoa!" She uttered as some jock cut her off.

"Sorry," he mumbled and gave her a once over. "How you doin'?"

Noticing his sleaze, she pointed to herself. "Gay."

"No you're not." He swaggered.

"I most assuredly am." She tried to get past him.

He grabbed her arm. "You just haven't met the right guy yet."

"Dude, seriously."

"Just give me a chance." He smirked and attempted to push her to the wall. "I could turn you straight."

She saw a hand grab his shoulder.

"Dude, leave her alone," commanded a husky, female voice.

Allison raised her eyebrows as the familiar blonde approached and confronted the man.

"You fucking idiot."

The man loosened his grip upon seeing the scowl on her face and retreated to his boys in the corner.

Allison smoothed her dress, face warming. "Uh...thanks."

32

"Not a problem. Dudes like that piss me off."
She sipped her beer. "I'm Susan, by the way."

"Allison." She extended her hand to Susan.

"Sooo...I don't really know anyone here but
my roommate." Susan put her free hand in her
pocket. Her blue jeans were baggy in contrast to
her form fitting tank top. The black Converse
low-tops complimented her outfit.

Allison traced the rim of her beer can, face
still burning. "Neither do I...I mean...I know my
brother and that's it. I...I don't even know how
my brother knows the host, to be honest."

"The host's my roommate, Ted Spencer."

"Oh, wait! I know him! He used to hang out
with my brother in high school!" Allison calmed
herself and turned her body toward the other
woman. "So...you live here?"

"Yep." Susan sipped her beer, cocked her
head, and narrowed her eyes. "You look kinda
familiar. How do I know you?"

"Uhh..." she gripped the can. "I work at Cool
Beans."

Susan's eyes widened. "Oh yeah! That's
where I've seen you! I applied there today." She
composed herself. "Weird." She looked into the
crowd.

Allison checked out Susan's toned biceps.
*She must work out. Is she gay? She sets off my
gaydar.* She fished for a compliment. "Soo...your

house is cute."

"Thanks. We were able to get the main level unpacked this past week. Ted, that's my room-mate," she nodded in Allison's direction. "Of course, he was already wasted at five, waaaaay before the party even started." Susan rolled her eyes. "He's not going to find a good quality girl that way."

She's not dating him! Allison's eyes lit. "Sounds like my brother, Chris. He's always stoned, but he's the manager of the coffee shop, so I can't complain."

"I'd truly like to work there. It seems pretty chill."

"Speak of the Devil! Hi, Chris." Allison telepathed anger toward her brother as he approached the women.

He turned his attention to Susan. "Hey, you're Susan, the new barista." He stumbled.

Susan gave a start. "You're hiring me?"

"Hell fuckin' yeah." He was double fisting beer.

"Sooo professional, Chris." Allison covered her eyes.

"Shuddup." He turned his back on his sister and concentrated again on Susan. "Ignore my sister; she's drunk. Be there Monday morning; we're closed tomorrow."

"Sweet!" A smiled crossed Susan's face.

Allison finished her beer. "Sooo…we're co-workers now."

"Thank fucking God. I've been looking for a job since I moved here." Susan shotgunned her beer.

"Which was when?" *Now that Chris is gone, I can get closer to her.*

"Almost two weeks ago." Susan shook her empty can. "I need more beer." As she left, she flicked her head back and smiled. "Nice to meet you, Allison."

Seven

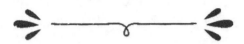

Susan retired to her room after meeting Allison. All that worry had turned to excitement, which led to exhaustion and a higher state of drunkenness. She let the room twirl around her as she twirled the opposite way onto her bed and fell asleep to the sounds of laughter.

She woke up to a hangover from Hell.

"Ungnerhug." She rolled onto her back and stared at the spinning ceiling. A welling arose in her stomach and she bolted to the bathroom.

Vomit.

I'm never drinking again.

Vomit.

She brushed her teeth and took some aspirin before heading downstairs. Gloom descended upon her as she took each stair. Empty bottles, cans, and cups lined the banister. Empty clothes and people lined the floor of the main floor. She sighed as she stepped over each person on her way to her coffee maker. *I live with an idiot. A loveable idiot, but still an absolute idiot.* Susan glugged her coffee and grabbed her keys. She needed something deep fried in healthy lard to calm her stomach.

The deep fried frenchee from the diner drove her into lucidity. Memories of the night flooded her head as she ate.

A girl.

A dude.

She put her pop down as she replayed the scene in her head over and over until she remembered that she was now employed at a coffee shop. She laughed as she turned the sandwich over. *Heh, so I* am *employable.* A wave of melancholy washed over her. *The job has very little to do with my degree.*

Still, there was that girl, brown eyes glinting in the light and a faint scent of patchouli. *I think she said her name was Allison. She said she worked at the coffee shop. I wonder what her story is. Maybe, we could become friends?* She shook her head. *I doubt it; I get along better with guys.* Susan thought about Allison's smile and it reflected upon her face as she threw her trash away and returned home.

The whole Monday shift consisted of awkward instruction while Allison showed Susan how to run the register. *I need to make it seem*

like I'm not interested in her as anything more than a friend.

"See," she pointed at the register, "this is how you ring in an extra-large mocha cappuccino with whipped cream." The buttons clicked.

"Whoa! How'd you do that so fast?"

"I have magic fingers." Allison grinned, but reddened as she realized that that statement could be construed as something sexual.

Susan smirked. "I bet your boyfriend likes that."

Oh, great. She's intelligent. Both a plus and a minus. She remained silent.

It took just a couple hours to show her the ropes. Susan had stated upon clocking in that she already had some cashier experience under her belt.

"Is it always this slow?" Susan leaned her back against the wall.

"Unfortunately, yes." Allison wiped a cup. "But we were busy the first week."

"What happened?"

"People just stopped coming." She shrugged. "It's probably because another coffee shop opened the same week a few blocks away from here."

"That sucks."

"You're telling me." She sat down the cup.

"Nothing screams 'job security' like an empty

coffee shop." Susan gave a half smile.

Sarcastic. Nice. Allison turned away to hide her face.

Susan stood up and placed her hands in her pockets. "Soo... what do you do for fun besides party?"

Allison faced Susan and twirled her hair, "Oh, nothing special. I paint and stuff."

"Coolness. Are you an art student?" Susan's eyes blazed.

She must like art. "I was..." She trailed off. *I hope she doesn't pry any further.* "You?"

"Naw, I studied English. I graduated a few weeks ago."

"You write?"

"A little."

"Like what?" *Now I'm probing.*

"Some poems and such." She shrugged. "Nothing spectacular."

Allison smiled and stood upright. "That's awesome!"

"My ex-boyfriend hated it." Susan dropped her head.

Ex-boyfriend? Maybe she's single, but she's probably straight. Her heart sunk. "What a jerk." *Oh, well, maybe we could be friends.* "People who hate literature are not living."

"You read?" Susan straightened her posture.

"Heck yeah I do."

"Who do you read?" She inched closer to her as Allison inched backward.

"Kerouac, Plath, Dickinson, etc."

"Me, too!" Susan jumped.

So cute. "You like art?"

"Yep."

"Any favorite artists or styles?" She was twirling her hair again.

"I like modern, abstract, photography, and street art. However, I like the classics as well. Michelangelo was a bad ass in his day."

"Street art?" Allison perked up.

"Yeah, like Banksy." Susan put one hand on her hip. "I like a bit of politics in my art."

"Eff yeah! It gives substance." *She likes street art. Maybe I should actually follow through with that artistic epiphany from the other night?*

"I haven't seen much around here." Susan continued.

Allison sucked her teeth before she spoke. "Yeah, Omaha's lame like that."

"Are you from here?"

"Born and raised. I spent some time in Kansas City, though."

"College?"

"Something like that?" She chuckled.

"Why'd you move back?"

Goshdarnit, I was hoping she wouldn't pry.

"I just got homesick, I guess." Allison smiled. "Why are *you* here?"

"I wanted to live in an affordable city before I established myself as a writer."

"Makes sense."

"Luckily, Ted's family is rich and offered us a house for cheap."

"That's awesome! How long have you guys known each other?"

Susan paused and counted her fingers. "About five years. We're besties."

Allison sighed and thought back to Kansas City. "It's nice to have at least one friend in a new town. That way you're not completely alone."

Susan cocked her head. "I know, right?"

Why is she straight? Ugh.

Susan continued, "You seem friendly enough. We should have drinks sometime. Do you know any good bars that aren't full of douchebags?" She laughed. "I don't really want to get kicked out."

They shared a laugh and kicked back for the rest of the workday.

Eight

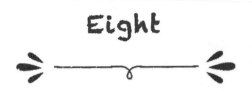

Allison went home and lay on her couch. The soft green velvet massaged her skin as she stared at the ceiling. Moments passed and she found herself back in that apartment.

Indian elephants stood on bookshelves and a coffee table. There were candles and burning patchouli incense scattered throughout the living room. The woman in front of her was a goddess. Long black hair, pierced nose, and jade eyes added an ethereal air to her vibrant personality. Her suntanned skin matched the décor. Allison was handed a joint and she took a few hits. She concentrated on the other woman's glossed over lips.

"Adia..." she sighed as she exhaled.

"Yes?" Adia whispered as she approached Allison's ear.

"I want..." Allison closed her eyes.

Adia was straddling her lap. She leaned in and grazed her cheek. "Tell me what you want, Allie." Her whisper sent heat throughout Allison's body.

"You." Allison turned her head toward the other woman. Staring at her eyes through the smoke, she pulled Adia closer by her shirt. She could feel her body heat through the thin layers of their clothes. Allison closed her eyes as she felt Adia's soft lips and a tug on her hair. She moaned and pulled her closer. They were enveloped in incense and heat as they fell upon the futon.

Allison woke with a start to a text from Susan.

I'm bored, wanna hang?

She swallowed.

Sure, where?

My place.

She was surprised at the speedy reply.

Alright, let me shower and get ready. :-)

Allison inhaled as she got up. "No pressure,"

she said to Mr. Scruffles. "She's straight."

What to wear? She meandered around her room for a few minutes after her shower before picking out a simple outfit of skinny jeans, a band t-shirt, and flats. *No pressure, so no need to dress up, right? Susan's just a friend, right? Still I should probably make myself look cute.*

When she arrived at Susan's house, she was taken back by how different it looked in the daylight. *Such rustic beauty, so authentically American.* She rang the doorbell.

"Coming!" she heard a muffled cry.

The door was soon opened by a very out of breath blonde. *What I wouldn't give to be the cause of her running out of breath.*

"S...Sorry...I was...cleaning." Susan caught her breath. "Please come in."

The living room was much different than the party. Many more breakables were in view and a flat screen TV was center stage on the wall. Susan went to the kitchen to pour some coffee. "Soo...what do you wanna do, Allison?"

You. Allison caught herself staring at her chest. *Dang it, I should have "taken care of business" before coming here.* "Just call me Allie." She looked at the TV. "Wanna order pizza and watch movies?"

"Sounds like a plan." Susan entered the room, carrying two small blue coffee cups. Setting them down on the coffee table and herself on the faded gray couch, she offered Allison a seat. "Please, sit down."

"Where's your roommate?"

"He's away on family business. It's a good thing, he's been a little irritable since he started his new job."

"A shame." Allison reached for her cup. Blue was a good color for Susan. It was calm and composed.

"What movies do you like, Allie?" She got up and went to the DVD collection. "I like romantic comedies and action movies, so I have a bunch of those."

"Let's watch a comedy." *Humor would probably calm my nerves.*

"Alright. Here's one where a guy tries to impress a girl with his dodge ball skills."

"Sounds good."

As the movie progressed, they moved closer and closer. By the end of it, they were borderline cuddling.

"Guys can be so stupid, right Allie?" Susan stated as the end credits were rolling.

"Yeah." She chuckled.

"What type of guy do you like?"

Oh crap, I thought she knew I was gay. I thought she heard me when she pulled that dude off of me. How do I tell her? Will she be okay

with it? She has to be. She studied English.
"Uh…The female ones."

"What a relief." Susan muttered.

Wait, what? "What was that?"

Susan corrected herself. "I mean, you don't really look gay but you are, so no competition with guys. Am I right?" She looked down and fidgeted with her shirt.

Allison gave a nervous laugh, "Yeah."

"Okay then, what type of pizza did you want?" She picked up her phone. "I'm starving."

"Pineapple. Shouldn't we have ordered the pizza *before* the movie?"

"Ha! I guess."

The next few hours flew by and everything seemed normal, but Allison was still confused. *Is Susan really okay with lesbians and what did she really mean when she said, "what a relief?"*

She spent too much time in her head. Susan soon noticed that her gaze was fixed on the wall. "What's up?"

"Nothing."

She narrowed her eyes. "You sure? You seem pretty out of it."

Allison swallowed. "Are you sure you don't have a problem with my sexuality?"

"Honey, I listen to Ani DiFranco. No, I don't have a problem." She rolled her eyes.

"Wait…are you gay, too?" She winced as

she realized just how rude her question was.

Susan paused before speaking, but fixed her gaze on the TV. "No, I dated guys, remember?"

"Okay."

Susan snapped back to Allison and gave her a hug. "It's okay to be gay!"

They erupted into laughter and felt the warmth.

Nine

Allison found herself staring at the multitude of illuminated cans of spray paint. *How to approach this? Blue? Black?* She bit her thumb. *Red and Black.* She reached out and grabbed a couple cans of each. Giving each a shake as she turned around, she spotted Susan down the aisle checking her phone. Allison scrambled to hide the paint and slowly pushed her cart down the aisle. *Please don't see me. Please don't see me.*

"Hi, Allie!"

Crap. "Hi, Susan! What's up?"

"Nothing. Just picking up a few necessities." She gestured toward her cart where tampons and toilet paper stood out in the open. "What about you?"

"I needed some supplies." *Must play it cool.*

"Awesome."

Allison twirled her hair. She hated this nervous habit. "Want to get lunch?"

"Sure." Susan gave her signature smile and Allison felt her heart pound.

Allison loved Sundays. *Chris never schedules us on Sundays. I should see what she's doing next weekend. Today, I want to commit to art and finally get this project off the ground. I'm just going have lunch with her. No bonding time today. No cuddling on the couch. No restraining urges. I can do this.*

She went through the motions as the cashier rang them up and handed them their receipts.

"Alright," Susan said as they walked out the door. "What are you feeling?"

"Indian."

"Awesome, let's do this."

The reconvened at a nearby restaurant and chatted while they waited for their server.

"Allison…Allison Stanek?" Said the waiter as he brought out the menus. "I haven't seen you since high school! How are you? Is this your girlfriend? She's just lovely!"

Allison shrunk into the booth.

"I…I'm fine…and no, she's a friend. How are you?"

"I'm great. What drinks can I get for you two?"

"Coke," stated Susan.

"Lemonade."

"Great! I'll be back shortly." He bounced away.

"Sorry," Allison muttered. "I forgot how many members of our LGBT community make assumptions like that."

"It's okay. I'm always mistaken for a lesbian anyway." Susan shrugged. "I don't know why. How is the rainbow community here?"

The waiter returned with their drinks and gave them time to look over the menu.

"It sucks. Sometimes you can't tell that it's a blue city in a red state, but that's Nebraska for ya." Allison felt electricity. *I know what message to use! I could make a series of LGBT graffiti art!* Allison grinned as she felt inspiration stirring within her.

"You have a cute smile." Susan cradled her head in her hands.

Allison sucked on her straw.

Ten

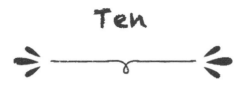

Boom. She looked the part. Black hoodie, jeans, black bandana covering her face and a can of spray paint in each hand. She got in her car and combed downtown Omaha for a shaded spot that would be visible in the daylight. *I need to be covert.* It took her a good hour to decide on an abandoned brick building just north of the Old Market that would be visible from the nearby interstate. *Thank goodness, most of the brick is painted white. This will help a lot.* It was a blank canvas. Her insides tingled.

She climbed up the fire escape to what used to be a balcony to a fancy restaurant. There was a walkway between the railing and the brick that was just wide enough for two people. It was almost perfect. Allison grabbed the railing and it let out a scream and wobbled. *Alright, I won't do that again.* She took out a piece of paper with her plan on it. *This first piece has to be simple. The rest will progressively become more eloquent and complicated. No rainbows for this one, just red and black.*

Allison shook the black can, looked around,

and took a deep breath. *Here goes nothing.* She stacked two rickety, wooden boxes on top of each other and then climbed. Praying that she wouldn't fall, she drew a ten foot diameter heart. After she filled it with red, she drew two, black male stick figures a la men's bathroom signs holding hands in the center. Above the heart, she drew in two foot tall block letters the phrase "Love One," and below it, "Another."

She surveyed her work. *The letters are a bit small, but they'll have to do.* She checked her phone. 11:30. *That only took thirty minutes?* She heard a trash can fall and bolted, but laughed when she discovered that it was just a cat.

Allison drove around the area to make sure that it would be visible. Pulling over to the side of the interstate with her hazards on, she could barely make out her work. Optimism took over her and forced her to smile and fist bump the air.

Later, while lying in her warm bed, she thought about the piece and whispered as she fell asleep, "See, Adia, I created something."

Adia lay on the couch opposite Allison's canvas. She sighed. "Come over here, babe."

Allison dipped her brush into the paint and pressed it to the cloth, "Not now, I'm in the flow."

Fire was in her heart and in her eyes. This is definitely an "A+" painting. It had to be an abstract interpretation of an emotion. The luck of the draw gave her "complacency." She painted a yellow circle and lines that faded from green into blue radiating from it.

Adia groaned. "You should be over here flowing with me, not paint."

Allison sucked her teeth. "You know art's my passion." Her eyes never left the canvas.

"I should be your passion." Adia got up, long hair sending ripples through the air as she tread closer to the other woman. She wrapped her arms around her, patchouli overtaking Allison's senses. She kissed the nape of her neck. Allison lost her concentration and surrendered.

"It's okay to take a break, Allie. You're not really creating anything, anyway. You're just going off your teacher's rules." She cradled her closer and stroked her cheek. "You should create your own rules, babe."

Allison looked into her green eyes. "I suppose you're right, but the deadline is tomorrow." She escaped and returned to the painting.

"I hate it. I hate the damn painting."

"B...but I thought you liked my art."

"I do, but it takes up too much of your time." Adia crossed her arms and returned to the couch. "We never see each other anymore."

Allison held her brush in the air, green paint dripping onto the floor. "We see each other every night."

Adia started sniffling.

Allison softened. "Babe, don't cry." She dropped the brush and went to her girlfriend's side.

"I...just...don't think...you care anymore, Allie." Adia grabbed Allison's collar and sobbed.

Allison held her closer, "That's not true." She kissed her hair and laid her head on hers. The painting faded from her mind.

She woke thirty minutes before her shift started and scrambled to get ready. The first thing she heard when she turned on the radio was a stupid pop song before the news.

"Yeah, Bob, religious leaders are outraged about this public defacement."

Score!

"I checked the station's Facebook page and there have been some heated debates about this vandalism. Local authorities are still stumped as to who could have done this and they ask that anybody who may have information to call crime stoppers.

I'm a wanted criminal! Allison burst into a fit of laughter.

She walked into the shop all smiles.

"What's up, Allie?" Susan shouted as she prepared some decaf coffee.

"Not much."

"Why so happy?"

"Oh, I'm just glad it's sunny!" Allison twirled.

"I want whatever you're on." Susan cocked an eyebrow and turned on the espresso machine. "I need coffee," she yawned. "I missed you last night. Ted left and I was bored."

I've upset her! "I'm sorry. I had chores and a hungry cat to feed."

Susan noticed the sad look on Allison's face and said. "Don't sweat it." She flicked her hand. "I'm just teasing." She put some dishes in the sink. "Yesterday you mentioned that the LGBT scene here sucks." She turned on the water. "Well, I checked my Facebook this morning, and the local news stations were reporting that someone spray painted a big gay painting on the side of some old building downtown." She added some soap and started scrubbing. "You hear about that?"

"Yeah, some radio guy announced it on my drive here."

Susan chuckled. "I wonder how many conservatives are going to freak out."

"Probably a lot." Allison grabbed a towel. "Maybe the Westboro Baptist Church will pay us a visit." *Maybe I should say "God loves fags" in my next piece?*

"Those people are a bunch of freaks, dude." Susan pointed a soap-covered finger at her. "I betcha anything that Fred Phelps is gay."

"Ha! He's so far in the closet, he doesn't know that leisure suits went out of style." She set out some creamer.

Susan finished the dishes and wiped her hands. "When did you come out?"

"When I was sixteen." She put on an apron.

"How did you know you were gay?"

Really? "How did you know you were straight?" Allison smiled and tilted her head.

Susan remained silent.

"Don't worry about it." Allison twirled her hand. "I've just been asked that so many times that I've developed an automatic response to it." She leaned against the counter and perked, "It's great to be straight!"

Susan cracked up. "Man, you're funny as shit, Allie."

This warmed Allison and she was in a happy daze throughout her shift.

Eleven

Allison decided to wait until the next Sunday for the second installment of her art series so that the police wouldn't become too suspicious. She lit some candles and cradled her cat on the couch. Her phone rang. It was Susan. Anxiety gnawed at her. *Why is she calling?* She let it ring twice before answering. "What's up?"

"Not much. What are you doing?"

"Petting my cat."

"Uh, well…"

"N…not like that!"

"I was going to say…" Susan paused. "They have toys for that, you know."

Allison visualized Susan using a vibrator. "Stop!"

"Okay, okay. Anyway, I was wondering if you wanted to check out this open mic night at this coffee shop."

"But we work at a coffee shop." She whined.

"Oh, c'mon. It'll be fun. Besides, I kinda want to generate ideas on how we can keep Cool Beans open. You're an artist; you're supposed to like stuff like this."

"Merr…alright." She rolled off the couch, much to the dismay of the cat.

She quickly dressed and left.

The coffee house happened to be their biggest non-chain competitor. *The Undergrounds* was located one mile from *Cool Beans* in the corner of an ancient brick building opposite a strip of hip restaurants and nightclubs. The sidewalks were populated by socialites and well-groomed men.

Why couldn't Chris have gotten a place around here? She parked her car and met Susan at the corner. Susan was wearing a simple blue plaid shirt and skinny jeans. *Positively adorable.*

"Hi!" Allison greeted the other woman with a smile as she pushed her hair behind her ears.

"What's up?" Susan's mellow voice soothed any anxiety that Allison had. There was a soft smile on her face that sent heat throughout her body.

But she's straight! "Nada." Allison noticed a copy of *Howl and Other Poems* in Susan's pocket. "You reading tonight?"

"Yeah." She took the book out of her pocket and looked at it as she flipped through the pages. "Just an excerpt from this." She held the book up and met her eyes. Allison was lost and touched Susan's shoulder.

"I'm sure you'll do great." She resisted the

urge to grab her hand as they walked into the shop.

It was crowded with soft lighting, quite the opposite of *Cool Beans*. The crowd consisted of twenty something hipsters. Books and acoustic guitars were scattered amongst the crowd as they awaited their turn on stage. Several attendees were holding beer bottles. *Beer? At a coffee shop? This is definitely something to look into. A coffeehouse that turns into a bar? Hmmm…*

"What are you going to drink?" Susan leaned on the bar and surveyed the beer selection.

"I think I'll have a PBR." Allison recognized the blue medal that signified good, cheap beer.

Susan looked her up and down. "You look like you *would* drink PBR, what with that floral dress and beret."

"What's that supposed to mean?"

Susan laughed as she grabbed her beer. "It means that you are a hipster."

Allison became self-conscious. "Uhh…"

Susan patted her shoulder. "Oh, C'mon. It's a good thing."

Goosebumps traveled down Allison's spine.

"Okay, where do you want to sit, Susan?" She scoured for a free table.

"Call me, Susie, hon. I call you Allie; you call me Susie."

"Alright," she said to her beer. "There's a

spot!" She gestured toward a clear table by the wooden stage, lit up by Christmas lights.

"Okay, lead the way."

They sat down and Susan looked at her phone. "It's supposed to start at eight, so we have about ten minutes."

"Do you go to these things a lot?"

"I used to when I was in college."

"Where did you go to school again?"

"Northwest Missouri State University." She sipped her beer. "You?"

"Kansas City Art Institute." Allison hoped that she wouldn't probe too much.

"When did you graduate?"

Allison traced the blue medal on her can. "I didn't."

"Oh," Susan looked down and then took a long drink. "It happens." She looked up and raised her bottle. "Cheers to life!"

Allison raised her beer and gave a half smile.

"Soo…Allie, why do you hate open mic nights?"

"I don't *hate* them…"

"But you seemed so unwilling earlier…"

"That's because…"

Allison was interrupted by an abrupt brush against her shoulder causing her to spill a little beer on the table.

"S…Sorry," said a male voice.

Susan's eyes widened. "Ted!"

"What's up?" He scratched his beard and pulled a chair over. "Mind if I join?"

"What are you doing here?" Susan shoved her things out of the way. "I thought you had work in the morning."

"I do. I told a friend that I'd see his band play tonight." He sat down and shifted his gaze to Allison. "You look familiar."

"I'm being rude." Susan pointed to Ted. "This is my roommate, Ted. Ted, this is Allie. I work with her."

"Hi!" Allison smiled.

"Nice to meet you." They shook hands.

Susan tapped on the table. "Soo…which band are you here for?"

"The Delicate Destruction." He chugged his beer. "My friend's the bassist." He sat the empty beer can on the table.

"Coolness." Susan smiled.

"Methinks he wants to hook me up with the singer." He chuckled and turned to Allison. "What's your story, morning glory?"

"I'm a barista."

"Duh," he laughed.

Susan rolled her eyes. "She's an artist, Ted."

"An artist? What's your medium?"

"Pencil, some mixed." *Spray paint.*

"Sweet."

Susan tugged on her jeans. "So when is the band supposed to play?"

Ted looked around. "I'm not sure." He spotted his friend and waved. "I'm gonna go have a cigarette with him." He got up and left.

Allison turned her body toward the other woman. "I didn't know he smoked, Susie. Your house doesn't smell nasty."

"He doesn't."

They watched Ted light up through the main window.

Susan shifted in her seat. "Soo...you never told me why you dislike open mic nights."

"My ex liked them." She internally winced. *I don't want to think of her. Not here. Not now.*

Before Susan could respond, their ears were blasted as the emcee adjusted the microphone.

Ted stood smoking outside with his buddy Zach before the show started. It was neither too hot nor too cold, and Ted relished the company. He had blown through a pack of Marlboros in a matter of days and bought a brand new carton. *Why hasn't Susan noticed the nicotine scent? Then again, her head is often in the clouds nowadays.*

Zach noticed him spacing out. "Hey, dude, wake up!"

Ted shook his head. "Sorry."

"Man, you've been out of it lately. What's up?"

"Nothing, just haven't slept well in a few days." Ted took a puff.

"That sucks." The bassist said as he texted someone.

"Yep." Two cars sped past. "Who's this girl you want me to meet?"

"Her name's Sam." He continued to text. "She does our lead vocals."

"Is she hot?"

"Not my type, but I guess she's cute."

"Awesome."

Zach's thumb flew across his phone. "She better not fucking be late again. Last show, her car broke down and we had to bail." He put his phone into his pocket. "Lost fifty bucks to some semi-shitty indie metal band."

"That sucks, dude."

Zach nodded toward a blue SUV parallel parking across the street. "There she is."

A thin, teal haired girl opened the driver's side and clacked red high heels on the concrete. She was wearing a black fitted t-shirt with a plaid miniskirt.

"Hello." Ted ogled her fishnet stockings as

she approached the two men.

Zach smirked. "She can sing, too."

Sam stole Zach's cigarette, took a few puffs, and returned it. "What's up?" She put her sunglasses in her bag as she checked Ted out. "You must be Ted." She turned to Zach. "Yep, he's a hipster. Cute, too." She bit her glossed lip. "Where are the guys?"

Zach smiled to Ted and gave Sam a cigarette. "They're inside. Probably in the back."

"Sweet." She lit up and smoked half of it before the other half of the band came out and told them that they were next. She snuffed it on the ground and grabbed Ted's arm. "Let's go."

Ted allowed her to pull him inside.

"I don't like this band." Susan turned to Allison. "The singer sucks."

"She's ok, but dressed a bit too hardcore. They're an indie folk band, not punk."

"Yeah…She is a tad bit too edgy for the genre."

Ted rolled his eyes. "Oh, c'mon, guys, she's not too intense."

"Yeah she is." Allison clicked her teeth. "You expect a folk singer to wear more modest clothes than a miniskirt with heels. Where are the skinny jeans?"

"Don't judge a book by its cover." Ted sank back in his chair. *Who is she to judge? Women are so bitchy sometimes.*

"He's right, Allie." Susan cocked her head. "She might be really nice, even if her voice isn't the best."

Allison pouted. "I suppose." She glanced at her beer and at Susan. "I liked that poem you read."

Susan blushed. "Thanks. It's one of my favorites from Ginsberg."

"I think you can write better." Allison twirled her hair.

Ted looked away. *This girl is totally flirting with Susan.* He looked back.

"Aw…thanks!" Susan wore a crooked smile.

And Susan is totally flirting back. She needs to come out already, for fuck's sake. He stroked his beard and watched Sam while the other girls bantered to the beat of the music and faded into the background. *Sam's cute, but she seems to have a strong personality. Not a bad strong personality, but she seems a bit too bold. Would she cheat on me?*

The band played their last song and Ted got up to get another beer. He was joined at the bar by Zach, who had already stashed his bass.

"Dude, we're having an after party. Come with us. Sam will be there."

"Ok." Ted shrugged.

"Ask your friends to come. Let's make this party bad ass." Zach slapped Ted's shoulder.

"Alright." He shotgunned his beer and made his way back to the table.

Susan didn't really feel like partying, but seeing Allison accept the offer changed her mind. *Allie is too pretty tonight. Her hair is too bouncy and her eyes are too bright.* She crumpled her napkin as she finished her beer.

"Let's go, Susie." Allison chimed.

"Alright, Allie." She grabbed her keys. "Ted, wanna carpool?"

"Naw." He put his hands into his pockets. "I wanna try my luck with Sam. So…"

"Gotcha." Susie winked.

"That won't be hard, seeing as she's all over you," Allison muttered as she got up to leave.

Susan got in the car. *Ugh. Ugh. Ugh.* She put

her hand to her forehead. *What am I going to do? I can't drink around her anymore. Something bad is going to happen.* She inhaled and exhaled. *I'm not gay. I'm not gay.* She turned the music up to drown out her thoughts. *I'm just confused. I'm straight. There is no way in Hell I'm going to let us be alone. Ted will help me, he always does. But, but, he's trying to get with that girl. Fuck.* She tapped the steering wheel. *Just be calm, just be calm.* Inhale. *Everything will be okay.* Exhale. *I'll find a guy to go home with and I'll be straight.* Inhale. Exhale.

She pulled up to the house and steeled her nerves. A thought passed through her head. *Maybe sex with Allie wouldn't be so bad. Maybe that's why it was never good with guys.* She shook her head. *I wouldn't know how to have sex with a girl anyway.*

"Doo. Doo. Doo." She sang to herself as she exited the car. She looked around. Allison was nowhere in sight. *Maybe she went home?* Susan breathed a sigh of relief, but disappointment shrouded her. *Allison's so nice and awesome. It wouldn't be a party without her..*

"Hey, girl!" came an upbeat voice from behind. There she was, brown wavy hair and all. Her lips shined with deliciousness.

Susan grabbed Allison's arm. "C'mon, let's get going. You took too long."

"Whatevs." She smiled.

Susan laughed and led her to the door, which she opened to marijuana smoke and loud music. There was someone shooting up in the corner by a fake tree. "Some party," Susan muttered.

"I don't really want to be around this," Allison whispered.

"Let's leave?"

"Yeah."

"Where to?"

"My place." Allison descended the porch stairs. "We always go to yours."

Susan sat on the couch and studied the girl before her. Allison sat on the edge of the couch and crossed her legs. A red floral tattoo grew its way down her calf and onto her foot.

Allison caught her staring. "They're mehndi flowers."

"What?"

"It's a traditional floral Henna design. I practiced Buddhism for a while when I was in high school."

"So did I." Susan leaned on her elbow. "Siddhartha Gautama was a pretty amazing person." She cocked her head. "He's on my top five inspirational person list."

Allison's eyes sparked as she got up and went to the kitchenette. "Do you like patchouli?" She reached into her cupboard.

"Yeah."

"Care if I light some incense?"

"Go ahead."

She placed some cones and sticks in the several burners scattered around the apartment. "I love patchouli. I have patchouli soap, incense, and body spray. I've been looking for a good patchouli scented shampoo, but I haven't been successful."

"Isn't that a bit excessive?"

"Naw, I just love it." She gave a slight flick of the wrist as she lit the last burner. "Plus, it covers up weed stank."

Susan furrowed her brow. "But we just left the party because of the drugs."

"I have no problem with weed, just the hard stuff. You see that guy in the corner? He was probably using heroin." Allison sat down and drew in her legs. "Do you smoke?"

"I haven't in about a year."

"It's been a while for me, too." Allison stared straight ahead. "My ex smoked every day. She was pretty much a permastoner."

Is she still hung up on her ex? She caught herself. *Why do I care? I'm trying NOT to fall for her*. Susan watched Allison sigh and cradle her legs. Allison wiggled her toes and turned her head to Susan.

"Adia was pretty intense." She glanced past Susan. "Were any of your boyfriends intense?"

"Like how?"

"Like magnetic, but manipulative."

Susan pursed her lips. "Well, there was Ben. He was kind of a player and liked to get into my head."

Allison's eyes grew.

Dammit! Does she have to have such pretty puppy dog eyes? "I broke up with him a couple months before graduation. I wanted a new beginning." Susan extended her arm on the couch and Allison fell into it. "Now that I think about it, not many of my boyfriends treated me well."

"That sucks." Allison moved in closer, enveloping the other woman in a sweet blanket of patchouli.

The ripples of nervousness did not break the surface as Susan rubbed Allison's arm. Allison slowly lifted her head, meeting Susan's eyes. Susan inched closer, meeting Allison's lips. They turned into flames amidst the smoke and rain. Allison turned so that she was now on top of her, causing Susan to fall onto the couch. She clutched the velvet to brace herself and put her other hand around Allison.

Allison moved her hand down Susan's side and under her shirt. *Shit!* Susan sat up. "I have to go." She sprinted out the door.

Allison knelt on her couch as she left.

Twelve

Ted leaned against the corner as his vision blurred from the screwdriver he held in his hand. The orange juice left a bitter taste in his mouth as he studied the half empty cup. He didn't want to be rude and not finish it, but he also didn't want to subject himself to such torture again. He swirled the cup again and looked out into the crowd. *Burnouts. Hipsters. Beautiful melancholy.*

He saw Sam in the dining room. She was handed a bag with two pills in it and then made her way to Ted's corner. "Hey there, Ted." She leaned up against him, her breasts cradled in his. Light streamed through it as she held the bag up to his face. "Wanna do some X?"

"I dunno." He sipped his drink.

"It'll be fun."

He felt her arm move down his back. "Okay."

"Let's go outside." She removed herself from his body and pulled his arm. "It'll be more fun." She giggled as she led him out of the apartment and to the dumpsters out back. She opened the bag and handed one pill to Ted and then popped one into her mouth. "It'll probably take a few minutes to kick in."

"Probably?"

"Yeah, I've never done it before."

"Why do you want to start then?"

"It's something different?"

Ted felt a rush of serotonin as Sam kicked the dumpster's wheel.

She laughed. "The dumpster looks real happy." She kicked the wheel again and grabbed Ted's belt. Her hand made its way down his pants. "Wanna have some fun?"

"Here?" He felt his body wake.

"Yeah." She pulled a condom out of her pocket and held it between her teeth.

He took it and pushed her against the dumpster. What seemed like an hour was only ten minutes and they soon made their way back to the party with grins and messed up hair.

Sam woke up with Ted in her bed. He lay there shirtless with his head buried into the pillow. She looked at him and then herself, also shirtless. Her head and body ached. She got up and went into the bathroom. Washing her face, she looked into the mirror. A tear formed and merged with the soap. She opened the medicine cabinet and took out a syringe. Propping her leg up on the bathtub, she took a rag and sectioned off part of her thigh. She inserted the syringe and winced with the familiar sting. *I should be used to this by now.* She threw the needle away. She took deep breaths as she made her way to the kitchen.

Ted was still in her bed. *I hope he didn't overdose. I don't need* that *again.* She sighed as she spooned some generic coffee into the coffeemaker.

The view fogged as she poured herself a cup and set the carafe back on the burner. She heard a groan as Ted woke up and crossed the living room, kicking the clothes out of his way.

"Coffee?" She held up her cup.

"No thanks. I gotta go." He grabbed his clothes, dressed, and left.

"Bye," she said to a closed door. She paused until she heard his car start. She sobbed as she drank her coffee at the table and faded into the scenery.

She came to around noon, just in time for her job as a waitress at the pizza place around the corner.

Ted left the apartment disheveled. He needed something to wake him up. Coffee. *I should have taken her up on her offer, but that would have been bad.* He started his car. *She's not the type of girl who would like romance like that.* He racked his head. *I slept with her...ugh...that sex was nice though.* He turned onto Dodge. *So was the X.* He drove around the city for an hour before pulling into a drive thru for some cheap coffee. His mind dwelt on the night. *Come to think of it, I don't remember seeing Susan or Allison at Zach's.* He shrugged. *Susan probably went home. Meh.* He looked at the clock. 10:00. "Fuck!" He screamed. "I'm late!"

He rushed home, changed, and floored it to work.

"Where you been?" His dad half yelled. "I'm backed up on paperwork."

"My alarm didn't go off. Sorry."

His dad sat down at his desk and put his hand to his forehead. "Don't let it happen again."

Ted walked past and heard his dad mutter, "poor work ethic." *Whatever.* He looked at the stack of paper on his desk. *Maybe some X will help me get through this shit.* He searched his pockets. *I guess I don't have any. Bummer.*

He sat down at his desk and turned on his computer, head pounding. Chuck sat across the aisle. He huffed and smirked as he watched Ted take out some aspirin. Taking advantage of this opportunity to annoy his brother, he took out a pen.

"Chuck, stop it." Ted said, eyes not leaving the PC.

"Stop what?" Chuck spun around on his swivel chair.

"The clicky pen noise."

"Oh, is it bothering you?" He continued clicking.

"Stop it."

"Ha ha!"

"Idiot." Ted winced.

"Yep! That's why I have a 4.0!" Chuck spun back to face his brother.

"Whatever."

"You're just jealous because you got a 3.7."

"That's still high."

"Not high enough."

"Loser." Ted fumbled with his paper.

"Naw. While you were being all hipster and shit, I got shit done last year."

"Dude, you're being unprofessional."

"Naw. I got swag."

"Whatever. Go do your work."

"You're lame, killer." Chuck stopped clicking.

"Fuck you."

"Ted watch your language." Their dad reprimanded as he opened a file cabinet. "You guys are adults. Act like it."

Ted looked at the clock and sighed.

Thirteen

Susan did not sleep. She lay in bed next to a mass of blankets. She stared into space. *I kissed her. I kissed her...* Her heart beat. *I'm not gay. I'm not gay. Why did I do that?* She rolled over. *What am I going to do? This is bad.* She clutched a blanket. *But it felt so good.*

She replayed the scene in her head at least twenty times. *Yeah, I'm not going to work today.* She picked up her phone and called Chris. *I can't bear to see her right now, but I want to see her.* She groaned, got up to use the bathroom, and returned to bed.

"Hey Mom, can I go to the game on Friday?" Susan asked her mother as she set her backpack on the table.

"Who would you be going with?" Her mother was slicing up some chicken for dinner.

"Summer."

Her mother missed the chicken. "Who else?"

"No one."

"You sure spend a lot of time with her." She turned around, knife in hand.

"What's wrong with that?"

"Well, aren't you afraid of people talking?" She gestured with her free hand.

"About what?" Susan took her math book out and began her homework.

"What if people think that you're...you know...gay?"

"We're best friends, Mom." Susan rolled her eyes

Her mom pursed her lips. "Hmm...Fine, you can go. Just be home by ten."

"Ten?"

"Yes, ten." Her mother resumed her dinner preparation.

"Ugh."

Allison woke up alone and sad. The previous night was a nice change of pace, but ended too soon and too disappointing. She rolled over and touched her lips. Her eyes closed as she remembered Susan's warmth. Just the thought of her soft lips was enough to get her out of bed, and the way she stormed out was enough to put her back. She grabbed her pillow and hugged it close. *I want to go back to sleep and dream it away.*

The cat jumped on her, silencing that thought. "Ugh, really."

"Merow…"

"Fine, I'll feed you." She poured some kibble into his dish and made herself some coffee.

She sat on the couch and savored the earthy aroma. *This is the best store brand coffee.* She half smiled as she sipped and ate some toast. Her stomach churned. *What am I going to say to Susan today? Maybe I should call in sick? No…I can't afford it.* She got up and pulled on the first outfit she found.

She took a breath as she opened the door to the coffee shop. He eyes widened when she saw Chris behind the counter instead of Susan.

Chris smiled. "What's up, Buttercup?"

"Nothing."

"You sure? You look like Hell."

"I'm fine."

Chris shook his head as he wiped a mug. "Maybe you should have called in sick instead of Susan."

"Merr." She picked up a rag.

Fourteen

Ted opened the cemetery's gate with a screech and a wince. Leaves rustled as creatures flew and crawled through the branches. He looked up. *How I missed the stars.* He stood for a moment and swayed with the wind. He grabbed a tombstone for leverage and stumbled toward her grave. The farm had been in business since the Kansas-Nebraska Act and keeping with tradition, the family kept the cemetery active. However, no one had been buried there since 1999.

Ted made his way through the tall grass, keeping an eye out for snakes, to a secluded stone in the corner. It was still shiny despite the tumultuous Nebraskan climate. Over ten years had passed since Livi died. Ten leaden years.

Ted groaned and yelled "I'm sorry!" as he threw the now empty bottle of whiskey at a nearby pine. "I'm sorry, Livi!" He collapsed in the grass and cradled his legs in his chest. His beard captured his tears.

"Hey Livi, whatcha doin'?" Ted sat on his mountain bike as he watched his older sister exit

the house.

"Nothing of interest to you, dork," she replied with a soft smile at the corner of her lips.

"Are you goin' out wit' Bobby again?" He rocked back and forth.

"Not tonight."

"Then why are you dressed all fancy?"

Olivia was wearing a smart but classy black cocktail dress that was tight in all the right places with a pair of red stiletto heels. She wore a little too much makeup for a seventeen-year-old, and a little too much jewelry, but she looked fantastic.

"Megan and I are going to the movies."

"Then why are you dressed like a slut?"

Olivia threw her head in the air. "Because sometimes a girl wants to dress up!"

"Yer actually meetin' another boy, aren't ya? Yer cheatin' on Bobby!" Ted laughed and rode his bike in a circle chanting "Livi's a cheater" until he hit a log and fell. Olivia erupted in a fit of laughter as Megan's Jeep pulled into the driveway.

As she was opening the door, she chided, "Now go in the house and make sure Chuck's not getting into trouble." With that, there was a rumble and the Jeep sped off, leaving a cloud of dust.

Mom and Dad were out for the evening, and

he was left at home to care for Chuck even though he was only two years younger than eleven-going-on-twelve Ted. He can take care of himself. Ted pouted as he went back inside.

"Give me the controller, you fucktard," Ted commanded as he sat on the carpet.

"No, idiot."

Ted stole the controller and laughed as Chuck got a 'game over.' "Haha! You suck!"

Chuck ran out of the room and Ted played for hours until Olivia returned home, laughing with Megan. "Megan, let's watch some TV in my room!" She took the other girl's hand and led her up the stairs.

"Livi, I don't know how you can walk in those heels!"

"I have bones of steel! Haha!"

"Y'all are idiots." Ted said, eyes not leaving the screen.

"Shut up, loser," retorted Olivia from the landing.

Megan was a tall cute brunette that Olivia had hung out with since middle school. She was pretty good at all sports and sometimes taught him some good basketball moves. Ted looked up to her much more than that low life Bobby.

Bobby sucked. He always picked on Ted and shot his classmates with air soft pellets. I'm glad she's here instead. He sighed and continued to press buttons.

Soon he heard giggling through the ceiling.

"Megan! I'm ticklish!"

Ted rolled his eyes and returned to the game. Minutes passed and he grew bored so he went upstairs to bother Chuck. He passed his sister's room and heard weird noises. Curious, he peered through the keyhole. Megan was on top of his sister, half clothed. That's some weird wrestling move. Ted shrugged and pushed open his brother's door.

He forced Chuck down the stairs to play on challenge mode.

There was a knock on the door.

Ted answered. "H..Hi, Bobby."

"Is she here?" the unkempt teen growled.

"Livi?"

"Yes, faggot." Bobby pushed him aside as he entered the house.

"Is she HERE?" he repeated, angrier.

"Yeah, she's upstairs."

Bobby rushed up the stairs, and Ted heard a door slam and some shrieks.

What's going on? Ted sprinted to his bedroom upstairs.

"I knew it!" Bobby screamed. "You cheatin' bitch!" The wall vibrated as Bobby punched it, "You fuckin' dyke, Megan! Fuckin' my girlfriend!"

Ted trembled as he ran to his sister. "Leave them alone, Bobby!" He screamed and placed himself between Bobby and the girls.

Bobby's long dirty blonde hair flew as he pushed Ted into the wall. Ted groaned. His shoulder hurt.

Olivia covered herself. "Bobby, I can explain!"

"You don't have to!" He said through clenched teeth. "I saw you two at the movies making out. Fuckin' dykes." Bobby put his hand in his shirt. "You fuckin' pissed me off, bitch!" He took out a pistol.

"No!" Megan tried to wrestle the gun out of his hand.

Bobby kicked her off of him. She hit her head on the bedpost and fell to the floor.

Ted threw himself in front of his sister, clutching his arm. He glanced to the door. Chuck was cowered in the hall. He focused his gaze on the gunman. "Put it down," he said in the calmest voice he could muster.

"No." Bobby took aim at Ted's head. His hand shook as he clutched the handle.

Olivia jumped up and pushed Ted out of the way. She knocked the startled teenager to the floor, but his hand slipped.

There was a pop, a thud, another pop, and a puddle.

Part of Olivia's head was missing.
Bobby was face down on the floor.
Ted cried and cried.
"I'm sorry, Livi!" he bawled as the officer pulled him from the room. "I'm sorry! I couldn't save her. I couldn't save her. I couldn't save…"

"I'm sorry!" Ted wailed to the night sky. He thrust his fist into the air and stumbled to the ground.

Fifteen

Allison sat on the wooden bench in front of the painting. It was a bright mess of oranges and reds with splashes of black here and there among a crosshatch of purple and white lotus petals. Squinting her eyes, she tried to make out the direction of the brush strokes. She couldn't and stood up to inch closer. When she was about two feet from the enormous painting, she looked around for an attendant. He was nodding off in the corner. She reached up and touched the canvas, running her finger up and down with the grain of the paint. Such chaos over something so simple. *Truly beautiful.* She saw herself among the interlocking colors and textures. She retracted her hand and cocked her head, her purple beret shifting with the movement. Allison narrowed her eyes and grabbed her satchel, trying to guess the title without looking at the placard. She focused on the lotus flower in the center.

"Peace," she whispered and looked at the adjacent white placard stating the name and a brief explanation of the painting. It read:

Peace by Troy Lovette
The artist stresses that it is vital
to be calm during hardship.

Allison closed her eyes and touched the painting again.

"I'm sorry, Allie, I have to," said the woman as she sat up in bed, pulling on a bathrobe.

"B...but, Adia." Allison rolled over on the comforter. "Please stay." A tear crept across her cheek.

"I have to. I can't stay in captivity forever." Adia walked to the bathroom and grabbed her overnight bag. Slipping off the red bathrobe, she dressed and opened the door. "See ya. Have a good life." The wooden door slammed.

Allison hugged her knees and wept.

She opened her eyes and stared through the lotus.

"Peace," she whispered again. Her mind now went to Susan and her positivity. *How could I be attracted to two very different women?*

Allison needed an escape from the crushing anxiety, so she went to Target. *Poster board would make this project so much easier, I could do stencils, like Banksy.* She set to work. This piece was going to be much bigger than the last, but still involve the same style of restroom figurines. Her use of red and black spray paint would be her calling card. *Unoriginal, I know, but it's recognizable.* She did love for the last project. She needed something different but the same.

Allison tapped her chin with her pencil. Click click click. *ENDA. Employment Non-Discrimination Act. This is definitely a hot topic right now. Each day there's some sort of news story about equal employment.* She tapped her chin again and looked at her cat. "Hmmm....End it with ENDA. How does that sound?"

She stenciled a woman at a desk answering a phone.

Sixteen

There was a stop and a start. Susan grabbed the railing as a hurried bicyclist sped past. She put her hands in to her jeans' pockets and lowered her head, wishing for undisturbed reflection as she wandered the nighttime street. She looked up. *I miss the stars.* She could see the lit up lofts of downtown Omaha. Lofts that she would never be able to afford.

A wandering piece of paper landed on her shoe. Pink and faded, much like youth. *I'm that piece of paper. Lost and faded. Allison's the only bright thing in my life, and there is no way in Hell that I can actually be with her.* She kicked the paper off of her and quickened her pace toward home.

She sat on her porch and leaned back in the worn wooden rocking chair. Bowing her head, she felt the wind whisk away a lone tear.

Her solitude was broken by a vagabond Ted as he opened the door and plopped down in the chair across the metal table. "You look peaceful." He lit a cigarette.

"Merrr." She opened one eye. "Thought you

didn't smoke."

"I don't." He flicked the ashes into the wind.

"What was that, then?"

Ted turned the cigarette over in his fingers. "A cigarette."

"But you just said that you don't smoke."

"I smoke occasionally, but I'm not a smoker." He tapped his arm rest.

Susan sat up. "Dude, you've been acting weird lately. What's up?"

"Nothing."

"Liar. I know when something's bothering you. Spill."

"Uhghh…The same thing that's bothered me from day one."

"Have you thought about seeing someone?" She strengthened her voice. "If your PTSD is acting up again, I strongly suggest you see someone."

Ted exhaled and snuffed his cigarette butt. "I'm not a kid. I can deal with this."

Susan opened her mouth to speak, but stopped herself when she saw the faraway look in her friend's eyes. Ted had left the present again. She turned her attention to the maple tree in the yard and thought of Allison as she too left the present.

Seventeen

Allison turned her phone over in her hands. *Should I text her or not? She's been distant.* She thought of Susan's blonde hair, the way she moved, her perfume. She gripped her phone and winced. No drug could let her escape.

Allison took out her spray paint once again and headed out into the night, this time taking advantage of an old tool shed on Farnam Street with a simple picture of two girls holding hands. She signed it Maria Libra in a half cursive script at the bottom and sped off quickly to her brother's. *Maybe I do need something, something besides art, to relax me.*

"I need a bag," she said as he opened the door.

"Whoa, what?" Chris let her in. "I thought you quit since you failed out."

"I did." She sat down in the armchair.

"What's up?"

"Nothing."

"Adia?"

Her eyes stabbed him. "No."

"Ok, then." He took out his scale from under

the couch and began measuring. He tossed the full sack into her lap. "On the house." He took some from another stash and loaded his bong. "I heard from her the other day. She said she needed to speak to you."

Allison was in the process of rolling a joint. "I have nothing to say to her."

"What happened between you two?"

"Nothing."

"You're full of shit. You two seemed so in love."

Allison finished her joint and stuck it, along with her new bag of weed, into her purse. She looked at her phone. "I have to go feed the cat." She got up and left. She didn't need this. Not when she had to deal with her heartbreak from Susan.

She got home and plopped down on her couch and lit up. As the joint dwindled down into a roach, she snuffed it, saving the rest for later. Her head spun as she fell asleep a few hours later with a bag of chips on the floor. It was not a restful sleep and she found herself awake at 4 am. She lay awake for a half hour and pondered all the bad decisions she made in the past.

"No, I don't think so," Allison muttered as she initialed her latest painting.

"Ah, come on, baby." Adia reclined on the sofa, reddish brown hair flowing over her bare breasts.

"I have to study for my history test tomorrow."

"No you don't. You're smart." She smiled.

"Thanks, but there are a lot of names and dates this time."

"You'll be fine. Come over here."

"No." Allison continued painting.

"What the fuck? You used to be so good to me."

"I still am. I just need to study."

"Fuck homework."

Adia grabbed her pocket knife and turned it over in her hand. *"I could do some damage with this."* She held it in front of her, examining her reflection in the blade. Then she placed it to her arm.

Allison put her textbook down. *"What are you doing?!"*

"Well, I'm worthless."

"No, you're not." Allison rushed to her side.

"Yes, I am!" she shouted. *"I'm not even worth your time."*

"Yes you ARE!" Allison cuddled her and kissed her cheek.

"Then don't study and actually spend time with me!"

"But I need to pass this class."

"Okay, whatever." Adia continued to press the knife to her forearm.

"Don't do it! Please!" Allison snatched the knife away and threw it across the room.

"Then spend time with me."

"If I stay here with you, will you stop doing this?"

"Yes," Adia grinned and kissed her.

"Adia, why did you fuck me up? Why are you still in my head?" she cried to the ceiling. Allison fell asleep to her tears this time, hoping the next day would be better. She didn't need any more reminders of someone she used to love, someone who used her love.

Eighteen

"What are you up to, Sam?" the man asked as he leaned in her doorway.

"Nothing." She let him into her apartment.

"I got a present for you." He took out a small bag of cocaine and waved it in the air.

She grabbed for it.

He took it away and shook his head. "Uh…Uh…Not yet." He put it back in his pocket. "I'll give it to you for free if you…" He licked his lips and glanced toward his feet.

"Oh, alright." She rolled her eyes and gestured toward her couch.

He sat down and she unzipped his jeans. She thought of Ted the entire time.

Several moments passed and he left. She ran to the bathroom to brush her teeth and draw a line. Soon she lost herself to euphoria and found herself outside of Ted's house. She looked down the street and watched his car darken in the fading sunset.

She knocked on the door and heard footsteps. Soft footsteps. The door creaked open and his blonde roommate greeted her. "Hey, uh, Sam?

What's up?"

"Uh, is Ted here?" Her vision refocused.

"Yeah, he's in his room." Susan gestured toward the back of the house. "You can come in."

Susan closed the door as Sam stepped inside. She led her to Ted's room.

The door was cracked and Sam could see Ted sitting on his mattress. She knocked, creating an echo of thunder in her mind.

"It's open," he shouted.

Sam pushed the door open. "Hey, Ted." She looked around. Books upon books and clothes scattered here and there. *Interesting.* She closed the door.

"Oh, hey Sam, what's up?" He closed the book he was reading.

"Not much. What are you reading?"

His face flushed. "N…Nothing, just a book about art."

"What kind of art?"

"Memento mori."

"What the fuck is that?"

"Art that reminds you that you will die" He pushed the book aside.

She picked up the faint scent of Ted's cologne and her heart raced. "Fascinating." *I just want to fuck him. Right now.*

"I have always been intrigued by the concept of mortality." He patted the mattress. "Have a seat."

Sam unbuttoned one button on her shirt. "You know what intrigues me about mortality?"

Ted cocked an eyebrow. "Death?"

Sam leaned in closer and ran her finger along his jeans. "Sexual desire." She nibbled his ear.

He unbuttoned his pants and then hers. She fell on the bed with her hands around him, gripping his back. She lost herself in his essence and sweat. It mixed well with her mental fog. The room was a cloud high above the earth. She landed with him on his blankets, panting.

They lay there afterward while he opened his whiskey. He poured her a shot.

Sam watched Ted put the whiskey bottle away, drawing her attention to the bare walls. "Hey Ted, I thought you liked art."

"I…I do."

"Then how come you don't have any drawings or paintings on the wall?"

"They're in storage."

"Why?" She sat up as he handed her a shot glass.

"I don't want to see them." He took a shot.

"That's…interesting. Are you that ashamed of them?"

"No…they're just from a different time." Ted put the bottle back on the desk.

"A different time?"

"Yeah, from my childhood." He sat back down on the bed.

"You haven't done any more since then?"

"Nope."

"Why not?" She tilted her head.

"I didn't like what I would come up with." He shrugged.

"I want to see them." *He's being weird...*

"Not right now."

"Ugh…fine." She flopped down.

Ted played with her hair as she fell asleep. "I love you."

Ted sat in the chair, its red velvet brushing his hand. The office was small with just enough room for a desk, two chairs, and a plant in the corner. A middle-aged man in glasses sat opposite him. He stroked his graying beard as he took out a pen and notepad.

"Sooo…Teddy," the man in the glasses said as he studied the tween in the chair. "Can I call you Teddy?"

Ted looked at the carpet; it was an ugly orange. "No."

"Oh, 'Ted' it is then. How are you, Ted?"

"Good," he said to the floor.

"That's good. Are you looking forward to the weekend?"

"No."

"Why not?"

"Why?"

The man looked up and then down. He wrote something on his tablet.

"I don't know."

He clicked his pen. "No school?"

"I hate school." Ted kicked his feet.

"I did too, at your age. Why do you hate school?"

"Too many rules."

"I agree. Rules are too lame, aren't they?" the man said as he scribbled on his paper.

"Yeah."

"Do you have a favorite subject?" He leaned back in his chair and crossed his legs.

"Yeah." Ted stared at his polished shoes.

"What is it?"

"Art."

"Why do you like art?"

"I feel free." He shrugged and kicked his feet again.

"Would you like to draw a picture?"

"Okay."

The doctor gave him some paper and crayons. Ted drew for the remainder of the session while the man filed some paperwork.

"What did you come up with?" the doctor asked as an oven timer rang.

"This." Ted showed him his work.

The man stared at it. It was a detailed drawing of a woman lying in a pool of blood. He took off his glasses and studied it for a moment. "Ted, who is that?" He pointed to the woman.

"My sister."

"Hmm." The man wrote on his tablet again. "I think we'll call it a day." He smiled. "Your parents are here." He led Ted out of the office. "I look forward to next week!"

Ted looked back. The doctor's face was no longer smiling as he chatted and compared notes with another therapist.

Nineteen

"*I don't understand why you are doing this, Allison.*" *Adia crossed her arms.*

"*I'm not doing anything.*" *Allison's voice shook.*

"*Yes you are.*"

"*What am I doing?*"

"*You're leaving me!*"

"*No I'm not! I'm going to class.*"

"*See! You're leaving me!*" *Adia chuckled.*

"*Stop being technical!*"

"*You know you will never make it big. No artist ever does while they're alive!*" *She laughed again.*

"*Dammit, Adia! I'm failing two classes because you can't bear to be alone! I'll lose my scholarship! Please stop this!*"

"*You're such an idiot! I'm letting you go to class right now! Damn, you're so demanding.*" *Adia threw a water bottle at Allison as she left the apartment into the cold rush of flurries.*

Adia saw the paint on the easel. She smirked as she smeared paint thinner around the canvas.

Allison saw Susan's car parked outside of Cool Beans in the gray morning. Her heart fell. *I need to be strong.* Her heart jumped, causing her eyes to widen and mouth to open. *What if I freak out? She probably doesn't want to see me.*

She opened the door and saw Susan behind the counter, her back to the door. Allison took a breath and walked toward the register to clock in. *Don't notice me. Don't notice me.*

Susan turned around.

Allison panicked and froze.

"Hi, Allie." Susan was curt.

"Hi, Susan." Allison began prepping some coffee beans.

The hour-long silence was overbearing. *I have to say something.* Allison blinked. *Be strong, Allison.*

"Susan, we need to talk," she said as Susan dried some dishes.

"Why?" Susan's back was toward her.

"You know why."

"About what?"

"You know what." Allison put her hand on her hip.

"This isn't the time, Allie." Susan picked up a saucer and wiped it.

"You wanna get dinner after work?"

"I don't know. How about we just forget about what happened." Susan turned around, holding a dishrag in her hand.

"Um…okay." Allison stiffened.

"I'm not gay." Susan shrugged.

"I know. You're right." She relaxed her posture. "We should just forget about it."

"Let's get dinner anyway. As friends." Susan looked at the floor tiles.

"…Okay." *Maybe all is not lost?*

The remainder of the shift was full of awkward raindrops and artistic pouring.

Chris came in to close up shop and gave them high fives as they exited the store. "Made up, I see? Good thing. I hate it when there's drama in the workplace."

Susan picked up her pace. Allison glared at him.

"If looks could kill." He backed away.

"Shut up, Chris." She slammed the door behind her.

Susan was standing underneath the awning next door. "Where are we going?"

"Is that one Indian place okay?" Allison put her hands into her pocket.

"The one where your waiter friend works?" Susan made her way to her car.

"Yes." Allison gestured to her own car.

"Would you like me to drive?" She clenched her fist inside her pocket. *What the hell am I doing? Why can't I think before I speak?*

"Okay." She opened the passenger side door.

They sped off with only the rain as music.

"I just don't think I'm gay, Allie." Susan poked at her tikka marsala and rice.

"Ok." Allie looked down.

"I mean," Susan's voice rose half an octave. "Not that you're unattractive. If I liked girls, I'd totally be into you." She smiled. "You're sweet, kind, and funny." Susan twisted her napkin in her lap.

"Thank you." Allison smiled. "Would you like to get drinks after this?"

That was a fake smile. "It's only six."

"Yeah…"

"That's too early, Allie." Susan forced a laugh.

"I know. I might still go out." Allison took a small bite

"Why?"

"I just feel like it." She shrugged.

"You should let me go with you." Susan flagged down the waiter for the check.

"You don't have to do that."

"I know, I just don't want you to drink alone. It's dangerous."

"Ok. Fine." Allison huffed and tossed her napkin on the table. "But, I need to change clothes first."

"That's fine. I'm just going to wear this. It's not too grubby." Susan smiled. *What am I doing? I swore that I wouldn't drink with her again.*

They paid their checks and left.

Allison stood in front of the mirror, fidgeting with her dress. Susan sat in the corner flipping through a magazine.

She watched Allison from the corner of her eye. Her eyes moved from toe to head and back again. She blinked and snapped back to her magazine. So adorable. Her eyes wandered back to Allison's wonderful calves, tracing her leg tattoo in her mind.

Allison caught her staring and blushed.

"Uh, do I look okay?"

"You look fine."

Allison twirled. "You sure? I feel like something's missing."

"Maybe a necklace?"

"Hmm…maybe. Which one would match this outfit?"

"The purple one."

Allison put on the necklace and turned around. *She looks stunning.* Susan gripped her jeans and relaxed her fingers. "Where do you want to go, Allie?"

"I don't know. Where do *you* want to go?" Allison ran to check her makeup in the mirror.

"Hmm…what about that place around the corner? It has a cool patio with some trees."

Allison ran out of the bathroom and looked out the window. "It looks like it quit raining. We can walk."

"Alright, let's get going." Susan held the door for her. *She looks so delicious. I just want a taste.* Susan shut the door, locking it from the inside. *No. I can't.*

The bar was a small, rectangular block with chipping burgundy and white painted bricks. There was an apartment above that looked almost abandoned. A group of men stood outside the faded brown door, smoking cigarettes and bitching. They quieted as the girls passed by. Susan could feel them undressing her with their eyes as she opened the door. *Perverts.* The two girls were greeted by a rush of alcoholic air and dingy carpet.

"Well, at least the bar looks clean," she

whispered to Allison as they sat on black bar-stools.

Allison suppressed a chuckle. "I'll get the first round, Susie."

"You don't have to; I can pay for my own drinks," Susan protested.

"Really, I made you feel awkward the other night. Let me." Allison tilted her head.

Honestly, I should be buying her drinks. I pulled a bitch move and left after leading her on. "No, I was a bitch. I'll buy."

"Hey, ladies!" said a sleazy voice from behind. "Why are you fighting over who pays?" He staggered a step backward. "I'll pay." He laid a twenty on the bar and put his hand around Allison's waist.

"Hey, dude. Stop." Susan removed his hand from Allison.

"Why? She looks like she needs a good guy to take care of her." He kissed her cheek. Allison squirmed.

What the fuck is up with this guy? I need to do something. Damn it! Allison's too pretty for her own good! "No she doesn't." She locked eyes with the creep.

"Why's that? She a dyke?" His voice rose, grabbing the attention from the bartender.

Susan got up and locked eyes with him. "Leave her alone or you'll have to deal with me."

She cracked her knuckles. She looked him over. "I could probably bench press your weight."

"I'd like to see you try, bitch."

Susan lunged, but was interrupted by the bartender. "Hey, now," he said and looked at both of them. "I don't want any trouble." He glanced at Allison. There was a flicker in his eye. Then he pulled the guy away from her. "Bill, I'm going to have to ask you to leave. You're too drunk." He waved some strong-armed friends down and had them escort Bill out of the bar.

He turned back to Susan and Allison. "Sorry 'bout that. He's a notorious creeper." He went back behind the bar and wiped two glasses. "Two beers on the house, ladies." He poured them a couple drafts and set them on paper coasters. "Also, he left his money." He grinned. "You guys just made twenty bucks." He slid the money toward them.

"That was…irritating." Susan took a drink.

"Yeah. He has problems." The bartender raised his eyebrows. "He comes here a lot. I need to ban him." He wiped the bar. "I'm Luke, by the way." Luke smiled and turned to Allison. "You look really familiar, miss." He stroked his beard. "Did you go to college in Kansas City?"

"Yeah…" Allison shifted in her seat.

"I knew it!" He set down his rag. "Let me see, if I remember correctly." He clasped his chin in his hand. "Your name is Allison?"

"Yeah..."

"You probably don't remember me, but we had Advanced Drawing together."

Allison's eyes widened. "Luke Barcas!" She put a hand over her mouth. "Oh, my God! *Why* are you in Omaha?"

"I moved here after graduation to work on my art."

"I always thought your drawing was amazing!"

"Not as good as yours, though." He laughed. "I mean, you were the best in the class!"

Allison blushed.

Susan felt heat rise in her face. *She's so cute when she blushes.*

"You stopped attending class, though. Why?"

"I was in a bad place." Allison looked away.

"Man that sucks." He got Susan another beer. "I see you got another girlfriend, Allison."

Allison blushed again. "She's not my girlfriend."

"That's too bad! Heh heh. You guys make a cute couple. She's much cuter than that bitch you were dating."

This time it was Susan who blushed. She continued to drink her beer. *Do I look gay or something?*

110

"You know Adia?" Allison narrowed her eyes.

"Who *doesn't* know Adia? She was kind of a player before she met you." He opened a beer for a woman next to them. "I ran around with a bunch of lesbians back in college. She slept with pretty much every one of them. Adia has issues." Luke shook his head and wiped the bar. "It's too bad; you could have been top of your graduating class and gotten your own gallery." He gave her another free beer. "So what do you do, now?"

"I work at a coffee shop with Susan." She put her hand on Susan's shoulder, warming the spot her hand touched.

"Which one?"

"Cool Beans."

"Never been there. Where is it?"

"Just outside the Old Market. It's kind of a hole in the wall."

"I'll have to check it out."

"Please do; it's never busy. My brother owns it." Allison leaned on the bar.

"Chris?" He wiped a glass.

"How do you know my brother?" She sat up again.

Luke looked around and leaned in close. "He's my dealer."

Susan let out a loud laugh. "Seriously, dude, the coffee is amazing and I want to keep my job."

Luke laughed and shook his head. "The economy's so fucked up right now." He sighed. "Haven't sold a piece yet." He set down a glass in front of Allison. "I'd buy one of yours though." He wiped his hands again.

Allison sipped on her beer. "Maybe I could talk to Chris and see if we can show your work. Even if we're slow, the more exposure you get, the better."

"Truth." He served another one of the other patrons. "That one street artist sure is getting awesome exposure."

"The one with all the gay pieces?" the patron asked. "That fag can go fuck himself." He took his shot and left to join his friends.

Luke sighed again and rolled his eyes. "I'd *so* much rather sell art for a living."

Allison turned to Susan. "I'm feeling kinda buzzed."

"Already?" Susan set her drink down. "It's not even nine."

"I know." She laughed. "Wanna go watch a movie at my place? I don't want to have a hangover tomorrow at work."

"Uh…sure." *Really?* Susan's heart raced as she got up from the loose stool. *It's okay; we're just watching a movie.*

Allison tried to pay, but Luke just waved her

card away. She tipped and left the bar wrapped on Susan's arm. Susan could feel Allison's face grace her shoulder. She swallowed as they passed another group of smokers.

When they reached the apartment, Allison swung the door open and hurried to light some patchouli as Susan sat down on the couch. "What movie do you want to watch, Allie?"

"None." Allison sat down beside her and laid her hand on Susan's thigh.

Susan still felt a little warm from the beer and saw only Allison as she moved in closer. She was pretty sure that the other woman could hear her heart beating through her shirt. *Oh my God, she's going to kiss me.* She stiffened as Allison moved in even closer and laid her head on her shoulder, promptly falling asleep.

Twenty

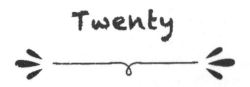

The morning was bright with a slight musk to it as Susan left the apartment. The aroma complemented the rustic brick and wrought iron fire escapes. A few birds flew from a nearby garbage can into the clouds. Susan watched them for a moment and walked to her car, past the parking meters and into the polluted gravel parking lot. She drew her arms inward as she sped up her pace. Her stomach was still a doughnut when she opened the car door. She thought of Allison, who was still asleep on the couch, and slammed her fist into the steering wheel.

"Motherfuck!" she screamed. *I just left her there.* She looked up at the apartment building. *I'm no better than a one-night stand. I should go back, but...but I locked the door. I'm an idiot and a jerk. God damn it.* She turned her keys and swerved out of the parking lot.

Ted was brushing his teeth when he heard

Susan slam the front door and run up to her room. He took a step outside the bathroom and heard soft sobs. His heart panged. *What's up with her?* He set his toothbrush down and went upstairs.

"Susan." He knocked on the door. "Are you okay?"

"Yes," she replied with staged composure.

"Do you want to talk?" His ear was to the wooden door.

"No." There was a pause between sobs.

"Well, I'm here if you need me."

"Okay."

Ted shrugged with gentle sadness. He looked in the mirror. *It's really hard to help if her if she won't talk.* He returned to the bathroom and trimmed his beard.

"Hmm…" He hummed as he stroked his chin. *Maybe I should talk to Allison?* He put away the shears and spritzed some cologne. *It's going to have to wait until after work or tomorrow.* He went to his bedroom and took a swig of whiskey as he put on a stocking cap. Ted looked at his bed and imagined Sam entangled with the sheets. He grinned and did a hop step as he grabbed his phone and left for work.

It was gridlock traffic on Dodge Street as usual. *Why didn't I take the interstate?* He tapped his fingers on the wheel.

"The vigilante artist struck again, Bob," Ted heard as he turned up the radio.

"Vigilante artist, Steve? More like art ninja, am I right?" The two announcers laughed.

"Anyway, folks, the police are still looking for this ninja, so if you see any suspicious activity, please report it. But hey, it's exciting, right? A Banksy-like artist here in Nebraska. Nebraska!" Bob chuckled again. "Anyway, more music in a few."

Ted turned down the volume as annoying ads filled his car. He lit a cigarette and took a shot of whiskey before the traffic moved again. He saw a billboard advertising a charity for soldiers returning home from war with mental scars. He took another shot. *It's not just soldiers that are fucked up.*

Traffic stopped again and he stared straight ahead as he drifted off amid the clouds.

"Hey, Livi." Ted rode his mountain bike away from the driveway as his sister parked. "Why are you late?"

"I'm not late." She carried her school bag to the front door.

"Yeah you are." He sat on his bike.

"I told mom I was going to a friend's house for dinner."

"Why didn't you go with Bobby?" He sat on

his bike. "He came by lookin' for you."

Olivia paused before she opened the door. "I told him where I was going."

"Do you still like him?"

"Duh." She rolled her eyes.

Ted followed her into the house. "Is Megan coming over? I want her to teach me some good basketball moves."

"Dunno. It's kinda late." She climbed the stairs to her bedroom. "She's coming over to-morrow night, though." She paused again before opening her bedroom door.

Ted went back outside.

Later that night, he got up to use the bath-room and walked down the hall. The whole house was quiet except for muffled sobbing com-ing from his sister's room. He tapped on her door and whispered. "Livi, are you okay?"

"Yes." There was a pause in the sobbing.

"Do you want to talk?"

"No."

"Okay." He went back to bed.

A car honked its horn as he snapped back to reality and sped off down the street to work. *I really need to talk to Susan or Allison.* He saw a red car and a red puddle around Livi's head. Ted hit the gas.

Twenty-One

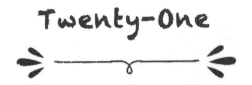

Susan refreshed herself and got ready to work. *Another day working with her. Ugh, what am I going to do? I'm not gay...at least I don't think I am.* She eyed the razor on the counter. *Well, maybe if I...* A few minutes passed and she shook her head. *No, not yet anyway. Is this how I should do it? What would be my finale?*

She picked up the razor and examined it. It was pink with a little stripe of green on the side. *How would I get the razor out?* Tapping it on the counter, she looked in the mirror. Her blue irises stood out against the bloodshot whites and puffy lids. She touched her cheek. *What's wrong with me? Why can't I just live?* Susan sighed. *All things are temporary, including me.* A shake of the head jolted her back to the morning. *I'm running late.* She rushed to work, not giving another thought to the razor.

The door jingled as she pushed it open and stepped inside Cool Beans. The familiar warm coffee scent greeted her. To her surprise, there were five customers in line. She picked up her pace and rushed to clock in and help Allison make drinks for a dreadlocked man and his hipster girlfriend.

The flow of people didn't subside until noon. Allison stopped and caught her breath after serving a girl with skinny jeans and *Tegan and Sara* off shoulder t-shirt. Susan found herself checking out the girl's body. *Cute, but not as cute as Allison.* She pinched herself. *I don't know how long I can keep this act up. Am I gay or not?*

Then it hit her.

She needed to apologize. *I must do this nonchalantly.* She breathed and steadied herself.

"What's up with the rush?" she asked while pouring coffee and syrup. *Yeah, this is good way to start.*

"I have no idea." Allison breathed as she went into the back for more beans, now with a bandana tied around her ponytail.

Adorable. "Allie, I'm sorry I left. That was bitchy of me." Susan wiped a mug, avoiding eye contact.

"No, it's me who should apologize." Allison set a bag of coffee on the counter and struggled to open it. "I shouldn't have invited you back. It was sleazy of me." She tugged on the bag.

"Here." Susan took a kitchen knife and slit the bag open. She put the knife back in the drawer. "It's okay. I like sleeping with you." Then she felt heat rise up in her face. *I should not have said that! I'm such an idiot.*

Allison's dark eyes studied her. She twirled her hair. "Well, maybe we should do it again? Hmm?" She giggled as she poured the beans into the espresso machine.

Susan started to respond, but was drowned out by the whir of the machine.

Allison stepped away from the machine and reddened. "I'm sorry, I should not have said that. I don't want you to feel awkward." She turned away and washed some saucers.

Susan excused herself to the bathroom and when she came back, there was another rush of customers. *Fuck my life.* She set to work.

Allison returned home that evening and cradled her throw pillow as she watched Mr. Scruffles play with one of his toys. *I just want her.* She moved the pillow up to her face. *I don't think that I can be "just friends" with her.* She bit the pillow and closed her eyes. *What am I going to do?* She rolled over on her side and saw the spray cans tucked away behind the entertainment center. *Now, it's not smart for me to go out tonight. The police are looking for me.* Her eyes wandered the perimeter of her apartment, stopping at a pile of sticky notes on the counter. *Maybe I should do something smaller, less noticeable, but still noticeable enough to keep my "movement" going.* She got up, walked to the counter, and picked up the notes. *These are too flimsy. I need something sturdier.* She tapped her finger on the counter. *Note cards. Note cards with package tape and markers.* Allison smiled as she sat down to brainstorm.

The next day, all around the University of Nebraska Omaha campus, there were hundreds of note cards taped to buildings, chairs, and trees saying variations of "Hi, I'm your friend and I'm gay" and "Hi, I killed myself because my mother didn't accept my sexuality." Campus police scurried to remove the cards, but not before the student-led newspaper got some good pictures. The next day, she made headlines in both the university's paper and the *Omaha World Herald.* Old men were denouncing her in their early morning coffee gatherings.

She checked her Facebook page and noticed that her news feed was full of her artwork and encouragement from her LGBT friends. Allison savored her morning coffee to the acoustic sounds of Ani DiFranco and lingering patchouli scent. *It's going to be hard to top that piece.* She smiled as she sipped her brew, all thoughts of Susan vanished from her mind as she envisioned how her next piece would look.

Her shift that day was busy like the previous one. It was strange how busy they became overnight. *I wonder if Luke had something to do with it. I need to add him on Facebook. I should talk to Chris about it tonight. I haven't hung out with him in a while.* She winced. *But last time I hung out with him, he mentioned Adia. I don't want to deal with that. Ugh. I* should *hang with him tonight.* Her eyes made their way to Susan's baseball t-shirt. *I wonder what she looks like underneath. I wonder if she's hiding any racy tattoos.* Allison caught Susan's eye and glanced away. *I wonder what it would be like if Susan caught me sneaking around at night.*

She clocked off ten minutes late. Susan was stuck closing since it was her turn. Allison gave a quick goodbye to her preoccupied coworker and sprinted out the door.

She looked up at the sky. *It's beautiful outside; maybe I should take a walk.* She glanced back at the coffee shop. *I feel bad that she has to work. I wish she could join me on my walk. Maybe we would kiss under the stars.* Allison stopped herself. *No, she's not gay.* She looked down at her feet as she opened her car door.

Then she noticed someone running towards her. She readied her mace then recognized the man.

"Hey, Allie." Ted gasped as he caught up to her. "What's up?"

"Nothing." She examined his jogging attire.

"Hey, now! Let's get coffee if you're free."

"Actually, a beer sounds better." She looked at his neon blue running shoes. "Don't you want water? Also, I didn't know you jogged."

"I do occasionally. You want a beer? Okay." He put his hands behind his head.

"You're not working today?" Allison walked beside him.

"I got off two hours ago."

"Right." Allison noticed his sweaty armpits.

"There's a bar!" He pointed down the street. "And they have happy hour!"

"Naw. Let's go to my place. I have pop, beer, whatever." They walked to her car. "We've never hung out alone. This is...odd, Ted."

"Don't worry. It's not a date. I just want to get to know you and I have nothing better to do." He laughed.

"Hmm..."

"Oh, I've texted Sam about this." Ted waved his hand.

Allison couldn't help but laugh.

Ted got in her car without buckling his seat belt.

"Dude, you have to buckle your seat belt. I don't have money to pay for a ticket." She put her keys into her ignition.

"Okay. Okay. I just live on the edge." He smiled.

"Right."

They reached her apartment and she poured him a glass of water with lemon. "You have a sweet apartment, Allie."

"Thanks." She sat down across from him.

"It reminds me of *Rent*." His eyes darted from the brick walls to the music posters to the art supplies in the corner.

"Thanks again." She smiled. *At least he has good taste.*

Ted sipped his water. "Actually, I wanted to talk to you about Susan."

Allison tensed and then relaxed. *I should have expected that.* "What about her?"

"She's been acting weird lately." He stroked his beard. "Hasn't been her happy self lately."

"That's probably my fault." She grabbed her coffee mug with both hands. "I made her feel awkward." She set her mug down after taking a sip and pursed her lips. "I kinda…made a fool of myself the other night."

Ted studied her and stretched his arm across the couch. "How so?"

"Well…I…kinda kissed her." She stared at the coffee table.

Ted studied her some more. "I gathered as

much."

Allison arched her eyebrow as she turned her attention back to him. "What?"

Ted leaned forward and clasped his hands between his knees. "Well you see, I've known her a long time. She's been struggling with self-identity since I met her."

"What do you mean?" *Is she secretly gay?* Allison took a drink of coffee.

"You see, her mother's kinda… How do I say it?" He paused for a moment. "She's kinda controlling. Susan was really naïve when she got to college. All her relationships with men fell through, and I always caught her staring at women."

Allison choked. "What?! She said she was straight."

"She says she is, but I just think she hasn't found herself yet." Ted looked down and then up again. "She's just like my sister."

"I kinda remember the news stories. Was your sister gay?"

He paused and looked her straight in the eye. "Yes. Susan has the same tendencies and disinterest in the male gender." Ted looked at his watch. "I should really get going, I have to meet Sam in a few hours and social norms dictate that I shower." He laughed.

Allison got up to get her keys.

"It's okay, Allie, it's not too far from here and I should finish my workout." He smiled. "Don't let Susan know I talked to you. She should work through this on her own."

Allison sat back down as he left. *What's going on here?*

Twenty-Two

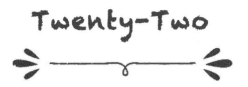

Susan got home and fell on her couch, groaning as she raised her legs to the armrest and propped up her head with a small pillow. *Why the fuck were we so busy today?* She shouted for Ted to bring her a pop. The echoing silence was the only response. *He's probably fucking Sam right now.* She laid her arm on her stomach and savored the air conditioning. *How long has it been since I got laid? Three, four months?* She allowed the ceiling fan to hypnotize her into a slight sleep.

"Hey Susan, come here," Ben shouted with a goofy grin while he sat shirtless on her bed, his brown hair just touching his shoulders.

"Just a minute." She spritzed some perfume on her neck and took her jeans off, revealing sporty black boy shorts, and stood in the doorway.

"You're sexy as always, babe." He got up and cradled her waist in his, sliding his fingers under her panties. He nuzzled the nape of her neck as she stared past him.

He laid her on the bed, and she closed her eyes, imagining someone else weighing her down as she gripped his back and moved with his movements. Back and forth. She opened her eyes and stared at the ceiling as he stiffened and relaxed.

"You come yet, babe?" He gasped as sweat dripped down on her face.

"Yes, more than once." She feigned exhaustion and cuddled him.

"Good." He threw away the condom and picked up his game controller.

She clutched the sheet to her chest as she fell asleep to the sounds of explosions.

Susan sat up on her couch. *It never was good with him…or any of my boyfriends.* She got up and fixed herself some dark roasted coffee. *Maybe I am gay.* She stirred in some cream. *No, just confused.* She thought of Allison as she walked back to the living room, imagining her fingers moving under her clothes like only an artist can. Susan felt her body wake. *I need her. Now.* Her nose could just make out the lingering smell of patchouli mixed with coffee that permeated Allison's house. Her lips remembered the softness of hers. Her fingers, her soft skin, her hair. *Oh, God, her hair.* Susan ran her fingers up her inner thigh.

Her cell phone rang. It was her mother. Susan panged with guilt as she answered. "Hello?...Yeah, I'll come home for the Fourth...Yeah, everything's fine...No, I don't have a boyfriend...Ted and I are just friends...I love you, too."

Her phone beeped as her mother hung up. *I'm not gay.* The yellow tile exploded with light as she flicked the bathroom switch. She picked up the razor and examined the light's reflection in the blade. Bending the shaft a bit, she freed the blade and kissed her arm with it. Not deep enough to draw blood or leave a noticeable mark, but enough to tear the skin with a slight sting. She exhaled as she hid the blade under the sink. *I'm not gay.* She stared at her reflection in the mirror, surrounded by light bulbs. Susan saw a tear run down her cheek. She ran her finger across the glass, stopping at the reflection of her eyes. *I'm gay.* She broke into sobs.

"I'm gay!" she shouted to her reflective audience and sunk to the cold floor. "I'm gay." She rubbed a few threads of the bathroom mat between her fingers. "I'm gay."

She heard the door open and close and rushed to wash her face. "Hey, Ted, what's up?"

Her roommate kicked his running shoes off in the doorway. "Not much, just gotta shower before my date tonight." He walked into the bathroom.

Susan heard the bathroom door close behind him and half ran to her bedroom. She turned on the radio to add ambiance to her sorrow as she twirled her phone in her hands. *Am I in love with Allison?* She closed her eyes as a slow song played. She opened her eyes and looked out the window, across the neighbor's yard, into Iowa. Birds swooped and rose with the wind through the trees and buildings. She floated to her bed and replaced Ben with Allison in her mind as her hand slid between skin and cloth.

Twenty-Three

Adia sat up as she scrolled on her phone. *What the fuck is this shit?* A picture of a masked woman holding a spray can was going viral among friends. *The eyes look so familiar. It can't be. Why the fuck would she do this? That bitch.*

The brick screamed against the concrete as Adia stormed down the street. She kicked at a discarded soda bottle and sent it flying into an alley. *God damn it! Can't she just leave me alone? She's doing this on purpose to hurt me.* When she got home, her lover was putting the dishes away.

"Get the fuck out," Adia screamed.

"What? Why? What's wrong?" The other woman retreated toward the corner.

"We're through." Adia kicked the doorframe. "Get your shit and leave!"

The other woman ran sobbing through the door.

"God damn it!" Adia slammed her fist on the breakfast table. "I need to go to fucking Omaha. I need to punish her for hurting me. God damn her."

She took her laptop out of her bedroom and sat down at the table. In an instant, she had messaged her friend Luke, asking for a place to stay in Omaha. She gathered a week's worth of clothes, some cash, some food, and other necessities before speeding off toward Omaha in her bright red sports car. *I'm going to make that bitch pay.*

Twenty-Four

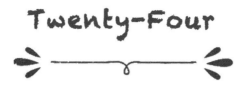

Chris flipped through a comic book as he listened to folk music. *I need to find a way to boost my business.* He looked over at the bag of marijuana on his desk. He set the book on the coffee table and loaded up a bowl. *This pipe needs to be seasoned.* Turning it over in his hands, he felt the cool, smooth stone. He placed it to his lips and lit it, almost burning his hands. *Damn! Haha!* He sucked in the harsh smoke. *Yeah, it needs to be seasoned.* He coughed and set his pipe down. Picking up the bag from the desk, he examined the contents. A pungent smell seeped through the plastic. He held it up to his nose and sniffed. *Good stuff.* He crossed the room and put it in a chest with the rest of his stash. The chest slammed down, caused the shelf above to spill multicolored leaflets across the carpet. Chris bent down and picked one up. He examined it between his fingers and felt the lamination. *A flier? Hmm...* Turning it over to see the back, he grinned again. *Fliers.* He let out a loud chuckle. *I'll attach fliers to my product! Haha!* He went to the kitchen and poured himself a cup of coffee.

I'm a fucking genius! He inhaled the fragrant steam and smiled to himself.

Chris took out his laptop, checked Facebook, and opened his word processor. *Maybe I should hire Allison to do this? Naw, it'd be better if I do it myself.* He found a couple of stock images on the Internet and saved them on his desktop. There was coffee cup in the center surrounded by text that read, "Buy a bag, get a cup for one dollar." He took another toke and grinned. *This is going to be so fucking awesome! He leaned back in his chair and saved the document to his flash drive.*

Allison drove over to her brother's house soon after Ted left. It was just turning to dusk and everything was covered in orange. She knocked on the door twice and heard slight creaking as her brother came to answer the door.

"Hey, Allison! What's up?" he drawled as marijuana scent attacked her. Chris leaned on the generic white doorframe. Allison watched as her brother's fingers tapped the peeling painted wood.

"Not much." She pushed past him. "Smoking yourself out?"

"Fuck yeah." He laughed and stood straighter. "Want some?" he asked as he cocked his head with a smile.

"Just a little." She entered and helped herself to a pop from the fridge.

"Alrighty." He rolled her a joint. "This is some grade A chronic from California."

"Coolness." She took the joint and sat down beside him. "I've been stressed."

"I can tell." He took a hit off of his glass pipe and set it down.

"Plus, we've been extremely busy at the coffee shop." She closed her eyes.

"Yeah, I know. Profit has been good, for once." He coughed and laughed.

"I wonder why that is." She put the joint to her lips.

"Because my friend found out." He grinned. "Awesome dude that he is, he put out the word to some friends who just happen to be my customers." He picked up his lighter. "For some reason I forgot to tell him I owned the shop. Also, a little birdy put some fliers on some bags."

Allison rolled her eyes and smiled. "You smoke too much, Chris."

"Naw." He took a hit. "Oh, I heard from Adia again."

Allison exhaled. "What does she want?"

"Nothing, really. Just weed." He packed another bowl.

"I don't want to deal with her again."

"Neither do I." He set his pipe down on his leg. "Damn!" He lifted his pipe. "I think you should stay with that Susan girl."

"We're not dating."

"Coulda fooled me." He laughed. "You both have that vibe about you. The vibe that unites the universes with a sense of unity.

Allison cocked her eyebrow and then furrowed it. "She's not gay."

He laughed again. "Once again, coulda fooled me. She practically sweats rainbows." He spread his fingers in front of her.

She bit her lip. "I don't like her like that."

"Liar!" He pointed toward her.

She looked at the floor. "Well, maybe I do. Maybe I don't."

"It's whatevs, girl. Do your thing." He laughed. "I'm so baked right now. I want cheese."

Allison laughed and drank her pop. "Let's make a pizza."

"Right on. I've got the munchies. I'm going to call a girl over because I've also got the carpet munchies. Haha."

"Ewwww TMI!" She went to the kitchen and put a frozen pizza into the oven.

He just laughed as his phone went off. "Oh, hey, speak of the devil. Adia just texted me."

Allison almost dropped the pizza. "What does she want?"

He tossed the phone to the opposite side of the couch. "You, apparently."

Twenty-Five

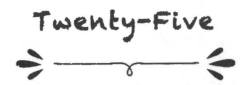

"I know. I know." Sam rolled her eyes as Ted reminded her that he had work in the morning.

"Then can we call it a night?" Ted leaned against the bar's brick wall. Its coldness pervaded his cotton shirt.

"Yeah, after the show. No after party?" Sam tilted her head and batted her eyes.

She really knows how to work me. He smiled and took a drink of his beer. *I'm going to regret this in the morning.* "Well, maybe we could do the after party."

"Sweet. I got some coke yesterday too." She jumped a few times and grinned.

"Good coke?" He lifted his eyebrows.

"Hell yeah!" She grabbed him by his arm and pulled him toward the green room. "I have about half an hour until the show starts."

He stared into the crowd. A woman stared back. He blinked and she was gone. *Was that her? No, it couldn't be. God, I'm so fucked up.* "Well then, let's do this."

"Wanna go to Denver, Ted?" Sam snuffed a cigarette in the car's ashtray. *That show last night was so kick ass. I can't wait to do it again!* She smiled. *I need a breath of mountain air first and some good shit.* "I need a change of scenery for sure." *And, you just can't beat sex in the high altitude.*

"Sure." He shifted gears. "I'll just call in sick for the next two days."

"You definitely need a vacation." She put on her sunglasses and leaned her head against the car seat. *It's been too long, Denver.*

"Fuck yeah I do." He turned up the radio, took a shot, and sped down the interstate.

I should probably tell him about how I left. She squinted through her glasses. *Naw, what he doesn't know, can't hurt him.* "I got the hookup there." Sam took out her phone and started to text.

"Hookup for what?" Ted glanced at her as he slammed on the gas.

"X, Weed, you name it." She waved her hand in the air. *I really need more of that shit from last night.*

"How do you have a hookup in Denver?"

Why is he asking so many questions? "Don't

worry about it." She looked out the window, eyes glossed over behind the tinted plastic.

"Sweet. I like surprises." Ted lit a cigarette and puffed, sending the sweet smell of nicotine throughout the car.

If I can't get coke right now, I might as well get caffeine. "Can we stop and get energy drinks, babe?"

"Sure, but I prefer coffee." He turned on some folk music.

"Coffee is fine." *Really, anything caffeinated is fine right now.*

He turned into the nearest Starbucks and ordered two venti lattes. "I don't normally drink Starbucks, for the record. This is just convenient."

Sam laughed and rubbed his knee. "You don't need to explain yourself, baby."

They were handed their drinks and left the parking lot to find the interstate. Ted rolled down the windows, blaring Bob Dylan as they sped out of Omaha.

The trees sped past the interstate and Sam inhaled the scent of the farmland as she and Ted reached Hastings, Nebraska on their journey west toward Denver. The air was almost hollow as it wound its way into the car through the passenger side and out the driver's, leaving stray grass in the back seat. Sam watched Ted as he continued down I-80. It was difficult to discern his eyes through his transition sunglasses. She squinted behind her own sunglasses and turned her attention back to the road ahead. *What am I doing?* She sank back into her seat and fell asleep amid the passing rows of half-grown corn and wheat.

A little girl in a pale blue floral dress and Mary Janes ran behind the barn, past the little goats, to meet Daddy for playtime. Mommy was at work at the office. Daddy was her everything. Gentle, smiling, Daddy. His teeth twinkled amid his brushy beard. Daddy was fun. Daddy would play games and they'd keep secrets like best friends. Mommy just didn't understand their games. That's why she drove him away from the little girl in the blue floral dress.

A bump in the road jarred her awake. Blue flowers dotted the side of the asphalt. She winced, took out her stash, and began to roll a joint. She pushed the seat back and put her high-heeled boots on the dashboard. Ted didn't seem to mind so she lit up and let herself float above the flowers.

Sam was so excited. Today was the day! It's going to be so much fun! She hugged her blue stuffed bear. I get to go to the zoo with all my friends! She smiled and stood against the orange brick school building. The air was crisp and cool with the sweet moisture that comes with spring-time. She inhaled and watched ripples form in the puddles from the running kids.

A girl waved at her. "Hey, Sam!" The girl came running toward her, pink coat unbuttoned. "Mrs. Smith has candy!" She grabbed Sam's hand and pulled her with a slight jump. "C'mon! It's the good kind!"

A group of kids assembled around a middle-aged brunette in a hound's tooth jacket. A wave of strong cologne greeted Sam as she took some candy. It was small and rectangular, the kind that comes in those cute cartoon dispensers. Sam smiled as she walked away with her friend. "Katie, these look like the kind my daddy gives me."

"Your dad is awesome, duh." Katie affirmed.

Sam smiled. Daddy IS awesome. "Yeah, he gives them to me when we play our games in the trees." She looked down. "I shouldn't tell my mom about Mrs. Smith giving us candy. Daddy says she can't know about this kind. She'll get mad."

"Why?" Katie kicked the ground and her shoes lit up.

Sam shrugged. "'Cause it has to be secret."

The next day, she was sitting outside the principal's office swinging her feet. Those monkeys were so cute! When I grow up, I just want to own a monkey farm. *She hummed to herself as the door opened.*

"Samantha, Samantha Flores?" The secretary appeared with a clipboard.

Sam nodded and stood up. She followed the woman into the office.

Her mom was there. So was a policeman. What's going on? *She started to tremble.* Is daddy dead?

The principal looked through her bifocals. "Sam, we need to ask you a few questions."

It was nothing spectacular, but it carried its own surprising nature. The star trickled down the night sky as the dust settled on the road. Ted was there with Sam as he put the car into park and opened the door. He kicked the grass, sending an explosion of pollen and dust into the air. He turned around and faced her as he spread out his arms. "This is it, Sam!"

"This is what?" Sam had her arms crossed and she watched Ted turn a half twirl to the trees on the other side of the cemetery.

"This is life!" He inhaled, closed his eyes, and opened them.

"I don't follow…"

"This is life, Sam!" He yelled louder.

Sam glanced at the gravestones. "But we're surrounded by death, babe."

"Exactly! Life is death!"

"Are you high?" She raised an eyebrow.

"Not yet." He sat on a gravestone and took a shot with a cigarette chaser.

"Isn't that bad luck?" Sam stepped toward him.

"Fuck if I know." He watched the cigarette smoke ascend to the sky.

Sam shrugged and took out a sack from her pocket. "If we're gonna party in a cemetery, we might as well go all out."

"You bring a mirror?"

"Duh." She drew a couple lines of coke on the mirror.

"Ladies first."

Sam pressed her nose to the mirror and snorted. Ted followed suit and kissed Sam as she climbed onto his lap. She smiled, her face inches from his with the moon reflected on her lips.

"It's like you're the moon and I'm the sky." He grabbed her waist.

"And together, we're shooting stars." She undid his belt and kissed him again as she removed him from his pants.

Ted tilted his head back as Sam broke the kiss and moved downward so that he had to rest his hands on the ground for leverage. Pulsating ecstasy enveloped him as her head bobbed up and down to the pace of his heartbeat. He stopped her and took her by the waist again, kissing her up and down her neck. He laid her on top of the grave soil and undid her pants. Her taste was sweet and succulent as moans escaped her lips.

"Please, Ted, don't stop."

He removed her shirt and paused, letting the moon shine down on her tattooed chest and breasts. Her nipple rings shone like stardust. He nibbled her breasts as he massaged her with his fingers.

His blood was rushing and he couldn't take it anymore, so he slid himself into her, causing her to let out a short gasp. They moved to the music of the night as they lay there in the little countryside cemetery.

It was a little after midnight before they reached the hotel. It was a small yellowish motel tucked away between the silvery skyscrapers in downtown Denver. Sam plopped herself down on the bed and watched Ted turn on the bathroom light, his t-shirt wrinkling with each movement. *Ripples. Ripples from everything.* She stared at the ceiling. *I wonder what ripples I'm leaving behind me, what ripples lay before me.* She looked at her feet spread across the bed and imagined that she was on stage, crowd roaring, lights blinding her as she sang a soulful melody. She turned over onto her side and set her phone on the bedside table with a soft clack. *Ripples, that's a good idea for a song.*

Everything that we do leaves ripples somewhere, on someone. She started humming to the tune of the melody in her head. Sam stood up and walked to the window, not seeing the brick building and the crowd of people from the bar across the street. She fingered the string to the blinds as she continued to hum, this time to the tune of the cars passing on the street below. Taking the notepad from the nightstand, she wrote a few lyrics:

Ripples left with your footsteps

from all the beds that I've slept
leaving no depth
in my death
from your ripples in my heart.

Sam tapped her foot in time with her heartbeat as she undressed. She walked into the bathroom and slid the shower curtain away from her, slipping into the steam and suds. Wrapping her arms around Ted's waist she hummed as she laid her head on his back. He turned around and smiled as he lifted her chin and kissed her through the water. Ted drew her closer and their hearts melded with the ripples from the shower's streams.

They woke the next day to the rush of cars and sunlight streaming through the translucent curtains. The air had a slight twang to it as they wiped the sleep from their eyes. Sam rolled over so that she was cradled in the nook of Ted's chest. Ted put his arm around her and drew her closer. He groaned and fell back asleep. Sam took his hand in hers and studied the fingernails and knuckles. *Hands like my father's.* She let go and studied her own hand. What was once so supple just a few years ago was now shrinking and cracked. She lifted her hand so that it was black against the sunlight and spread her fingers wide. *What am I doing with my life? Is this love real?*

She slid out of bed, careful not to wake Ted, and pulled on some jeans. Sam walked topless to the bathroom where she had left her shirt on the floor. She skipped the bra and pulled the shirt over her head. It was wrinkled. *Just like my life.* She smoothed it, but the wrinkles remained. Shrugging, she picked up the hairbrush and ran it through her hair. In five minutes, she was dressed and out the door. *Coffee sounds really good right now.* Sam exited the hotel and walked around the block to a small coffee shop half hidden by the busy intersection.

The shop was brick with blue paint and dark, wooden doors. She turned the brass doorknob and entered into a cloud of incense and coffee. There were scattered twenty-somethings and businessmen around the couches and tables. She ordered herself a caramel latte and sat in a patched green armchair and waited.

It wasn't long before he arrived, a lanky man with long black hair and scruffy goatee. He was wearing a red and olive beanie that complemented his brown shirt and torn jeans. He grinned as he sat opposite her.

"Long time, no see, Sammy." He leaned

back and rested his legs on the coffee table.

"I know, right?" She feigned a smile. "It's nice to see you, Kyle."

"How have you been?"

"I've been okay." She wrapped her hands around her paper cup.

"Just okay? That sucks, man." He took a drink of his mocha. "I'd have thought you'd be all over the indie circuit by now."

Sam shifted in her seat. "Listen, can we just get this over with? I have things to do."

"Like me?" He laughed.

"No." She thinned her lips. "We're over, remember?"

"Vaguely." He smirked and drew a small bag out of his jeans. Putting it under his cup, he slid it to her.

With the ease of experience, she slipped the bag from under the cup and into her pocket. "You seeing anyone?" She passed him some cash the same way.

"Yeah. I think I might marry her."

Sam scoffed. "You said you'd marry me."

"Yes, but that was in high school." Kyle put the money into his wallet.

"A long time ago…" She sighed.

"What about you?"

"I've found someone."

"Well, he's very lucky." He sat up. "I gotta

go pick up my daughter."

"Nice seeing you." She feigned another smile.

"You too." He waved with a genuine smile.

Sam chugged the rest of her latte and half sprinted back to the motel. *I can't believe he has a daughter. Since when was he responsible?* She pushed him out of her mind as she slid the door key and found Ted shirtless and still asleep. *He's so adorable. Maybe I could marry him.* She smiled and set the bag on the nightstand so that he would see it first thing when he woke up. Sam lay back down on the bed and checked her Facebook. Some ninja was causing havoc in Omaha.

"I want you to meet some of my college friends. Come with me to this house party tonight." Sam applied red lipstick as Ted slid on his Toms. The lipstick clacked as she set it on the counter.

"You went to college?" Ted observed her from the bed.

"Only for a semester. Not my thing." She snapped on some hoop earrings.

"Here in Denver?" *She's never mentioned this to me.* He raised an eyebrow. *I wonder what other secrets she has.*

"Yeah." She came out of the bathroom after spritzing some hairspray. "No, I'm going to invite you to a house party tonight in Omaha." She sighed. "Sometimes, you're something else."

"Okay. Fine. I'll go with you. When does it start?" *I meant her college, but whatever.*

"In about an hour." Sam put on a black mini skirt with a white polo. Sliding a red tie over her head, she sat down by him. "Kyle's picking us up?"

Is that her ex? "Kyle?"

"Yeah, Kyle. He used to be my dealer."

"Oh." Ted kneaded his palms together. *What would Livi say if she knew I was in love with a druggie. She'd be disappointed. No.* He stopped fidgeting. *I already failed her. I've disappointed her already. Any other disappointments wouldn't matter.*

Sam looked at his hands then to his far off face and back to his hands. She took his in hers and brought them to her lips. "I love you, babe."

"I love you too." He turned himself toward her and guided a stray hair behind her ear. *Her face is so beautiful.* He kissed her as she lifted her chin.

She pulled herself away after the kiss and took out her stash. "Let's smoke some weed before we head out. It'll make things less awkward." She pulled out her stone pipe and packed a bowl. "You start. I just got this pipe the other day and haven't seasoned it yet. I want you to have the first toke."

That's impressive. She usually starts our smoke sessions. She must really care about me. Ted grinned as he took the pipe and a lighter from her. He put it to his lips, lit, and inhaled. After a few seconds, he coughed. "That's kinda harsh."

He handed the pipe to Sam and watched her as her teal hair melded with the smoke. She exhaled in rings toward the ceiling. *She is one with the smoke. I am one with her.* He took the pipe and flew with her.

Sam's phone rang. Kyle. She answered and chatted for a moment before hanging up. "We gotta go, babe." She smiled. "This party's going to be kick ass. Kyle's got some acid."

"That sounds hardcore."

"It is. He only parties hard." She gathered her purse. "Too bad he has a kid now, but she's at her mom's tonight, so he's free to do what he wants." She made her way to the door. "Have you ever dropped acid?"

"No." *It sounds fun.*

"Oh, you NEED to. It's trippy, better than 'shrooms or E." She gestured to him. "Let's get going."

Ted grabbed his keys and followed her lead.

Sam was a few feet ahead of him as she met Kyle in the parking lot. He was leaning against a 1950's light blue Cadillac.

Classy. Kyle approached Ted with a warm smile. "I'm Kyle. You must be Ted. I've heard so much about you."

"Nice to meet you." *He doesn't seem so bad.*

Kyle held the back door open for them. "I'm so glad you guys are coming out tonight. It's been so long since I've partied with Sam. You used to get crazy back in the day."

"It's only been a year." Sam fussed with the clasp on her purse.

"A long year." Kyle put the keys into the ignition and started the car. "So much has changed. John's still around."

"I'm surprised." Sam shifted in her seat.

"Me, too. The guy's turned into a horrible junkie. He texted me the other day, wanting to know if I wanted to see his new lab. I was like, 'no, I'm busy.' Then he told me to fuck off, so I was like, 'whatever.'"

Sam turned to Ted. "John used to be cool, but then he tried meth. Meth is not cool. I've never done it. I like my teeth." She giggled at Kyle.

I'm not surprised that Sam knows junkies. Thankfully, she is not one. She just uses for rec-

reation. Ted looked at Sam. "I'll never do meth. Too trashy."

"Truth." Kyle braked at a stoplight. "We're almost there." Kyle glanced at Sam. "I've moved from the Highlands to a loft on Colfax."

"But you're not *gay.*" Sam snorted.

"I know. Isn't it *ironic*?" He laughed with her. "I love the area, though. It's got so much character and there's this chill ass bar just a block away. They've always got a good band playing. A different genre every night. Provides me with a steady source of new clientele." He winked and pulled over to let an ambulance pass. "Ted, what types of music do you like?"

"Indie rock mostly. Stuff along the lines of Bright Eyes."

"Coolness. I could hook you up with some autographed swag. I saw Connor Oberst live the other night." Kyle pulled into a private parking garage and stopped the car on the third level. He got out and opened the door again for the couple. "There's an elevator nearby, I live on the thirtieth floor." He chuckled. "I love being able to park *under* my apartment!" He guided them into the glass elevator.

Ted looked out at the Denver skyline. The lights flickered with the wind as the sun set behind the distant mountains. *So beautiful. I wish it was like this in Omaha.* He watched the rising

154

moon. *I wish Livi was here to enjoy this. She would have loved Denver.*

Sam turned toward Ted. "It's amazing isn't it? Omaha doesn't compare. I wish I hadn't flunked out. I would be partying hardcore."

"You could have stayed, Sam." Kyle stared into his reflection.

"No I couldn't." She looked down. "Not after what happened."

"What happened?" Ted put his hand on the side of the elevator. The warm metal contrasted Sam's cold eyes.

"I'll tell you later."

Kyle smiled as the door opened. "We're here!" He pulled Sam out of the elevator.

Ted hesitated as he noticed a crowd of hipsters swaying to Sarah McLachlan from a record player that was rigged to semi huge speakers on each side.

A girl with victory rolls and cat eye makeup held a red cup as she rushed to the door. "Oh my God, it's Sam!" She smiled as she hugged her. "I haven't seen you in forever! I missed you!" She let go and got herself another drink.

The room stopped as the three of them entered. It was an open living room that connected to a kitchen and bedroom. Not quite a studio, it had the feel that one could steal away to a hidden nook amid the bookshelves and old thrift shop paintings. The scent of marijuana and sandal-wood incense permeated the air, adding a surreal feel to the scene, like that of an old movie from the seventies.

Sam led Ted to a sofa in the corner. He followed, still mesmerized by flowing smoke and chatter. They sat down and Kyle approached with two beers. "Here, drink up." He handed the drinks to them. "I have some business to take care of in the kitchen, but I should be back shortly." He pursed his lips and looked away.

"Hey, before you go." Sam fished in her purse. "Here's twenty."

Kyle gave her a soft smile and a knowing wink. "It won't be long."

He left and they sat there in silence until Sam turned to Ted. "Okay, so what happened was..."

She was interrupted by the same girl that greeted them. "Now, don't tell me that you're going to spend the night here in this corner, Sam." She pursed her lips. "We've got some catching up to do." She wedged herself between Sam and the sofa's arm. "Introduce me to your boyfriend." Her eyes traveled from Ted's stocking hat to his sneakers.

"His name is Ted, and we're not dating." Sam shuffled to make room for her friend. "At least not Facebook officially." She turned to Ted. "This is Calli, my former roommate."

"Her best roommate ever." Calli smiled behind red lipstick.

"Yeah." Sam looked away.

"It's a shame you had to move." Calli pushed a stray hair behind Sam's ear. "I wish you would have stayed. I missed our nights together." She turned to Ted. "No, offense." She laughed.

What's going on? Ted arched his eyebrow.

"Yes, Ted, we slept together." She put her arm around Sam. "Of course, it was for coke, but still, the best lay I've ever had." Calli laughed again.

"Uh, huh." Ted muttered. *I knew it.* He looked at Sam's distant expression. *It's obvious she regrets it.*

"Anyway, I gotta find my person. Nice to meet you, Ted." She got up, swayed, and found her friend.

Sam threw her hands back. "So that's what happened." She rested her head on her hand, covering her eyes. "I slept with her for free rent and coke." She removed her hand and sipped on her beer.

She's so sad. Ted put his hand on her leg. *She's a prisoner, just like me.*

"Here ya go." Kyle appeared and threw a bag of white powder in Sam's lap. "I got you a little extra for your friend, since it's been *forever* since we've seen each other. I've got some E as well,

157

but unfortunately, I couldn't get those for free."

"How much for it?" Sam finished her beer.

Kyle's eyes flicked to Ted and back to Sam. "Let's discuss that in the kitchen." He handed another beer to Ted. "We'll be back momentarily."

"Go ahead." Ted sunk into the sofa. *I know what's going on. It's so sad.* He caught a glimpse of Livi in the corner. *Why's she here? She doesn't know these people. Then again, I don't either.* He raised his bottle. *I'm going to redeem myself.* He glanced again at Livi's corner. She was gone. *Why'd you leave, Livi?*

"It's 'cuz you're a failure," a woman joked at her boyfriend as they walked by Ted.

I know I'm a failure, Livi. You don't need to remind me. I will redeem myself. Just believe me.

The prairie never seemed as open as that day. The sun never so bright. The grass never so free. Ted drove back to Omaha with Sam asleep next to him. Her teal hair shivered with the light wind from the air conditioner. The heat turned the road into water as he swam the golden sea of Nebraska.

He thought of the previous night. How he

caught Sam in the arms of that man. He narrowed his eyes and hit the gas. *She looked so, so constrained after that.* He spotted a windmill in the distance spinning. Everything was spinning.

Spinning.

He pulled over. Sam was still asleep. Ted sat for a moment, turned on his hazards, and left the car, vomiting in the process. Kicking a mixture of grass and gravel, he approached a wooden post of the barbed wire fence separating him from the far off cattle. *We're all part of the herd.* He leaned on the post. *Cattle are never free unless they're dead.*

He relieved himself, lit a cigarette, and got back in the car. He reached under the seat and took out a shooter of Jack. He emptied the bottle and looked at Sam. *I have to free her.* He sped toward Omaha. *Two hundred miles to go.*

He dropped Sam off and went home, passing decrepit buildings and hoodlums. He sneered. *What is this "freedom" concept? Nobody's free. Not the gangsters. Not me. There is only freedom in death. The fallen gangsters were the smart ones. Die young, achieve freedom. Look at Susan, she's held captive because she can't be herself. Allison's controlled by her crazy ex, at least that's what Chris said at the party. Chris, by drugs. Sam...Sam...* He pulled into his driveway and parked. *Sam, by men.* He turned the key and looked at his whiskey bottle. *And me? I'm controlled by Livi's death.* He watched Susan through the curtains in the front window. *I must free myself. I must free them. I must die.*

Twenty-Six

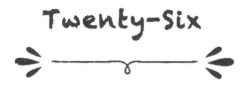

Ted arrived in Omaha that Sunday night. The leaves rose and fell with the intermittent raindrops as he walked up to the porch. He inhaled the fragrance of cut grass mixed with damp earth. *This may be the last time I smell this. The last time I open this door.* He grasped the brass doorknob, savoring the coldness, and turned it. The familiar smell of coffee flooded his nostrils and he put one foot inside, eyes closed. *I'm going to miss this house.* He stepped further into the house. Hearing familiar footsteps, he opened his eyes.

Susan was leaning against the aged wooden kitchen doorframe. "How was your trip?" She lifted a "number one grandma" coffee cup to her lips.

She cracks me up. Ted smiled. "It was good. Liberating even."

"That's good. I'm glad you enjoyed your trip." She crossed her arms.

Her eyes are frowning. Something's bothering her. "How was your weekend?"

"It was good. Allison and I hung out Friday

161

night."

"That's cool. How was it?" Ted started to make his way to the bathroom.

"It was alright. Her ex is in town." Susan went into the kitchen and set her cup in the sink.

Ted stood and watched her. *I bet she's hurting inside.* "That sounds horrible. You think she's going to get back with her and leave you?" *Oh, shit, did I say that?*

"We're...not...together." Susan came back into the living room and looked Ted over. "I'm not gay, Ted. Why would you think that?"

Ted shrugged and went into the bathroom.

Susan caught up to him in the fluorescent bathroom lighting. The blue tiled walls reflected her face and he turned around. *She seems much older. Much more distant. Where is her head?* "What's up, buttercup?"

"Are you ok? You seem like a different person." He could see sadness in her eyes. *I can't tell her anything right now. She needs to focus on herself.*

She continued, "I don't think I like this Sam girl. She seems....I don't know...bad for you." She crossed her arms and looked Ted in the eye. "Look, I just don't want anything bad to happen. Remember when I accidentally OD'ed on weed chocolate? I don't want you to experience that, much less with heroin or crack."

"Look, I'm fine." He threw up his hands. "Sam's fine. Just because she uses, doesn't mean she's a bad person." He closed the door and looked in the mirror. Dark circles were almost hidden by his glasses and his beard needed trimming. He placed his palm on the cold surface. *I'm ravaged by the prison. I'm no better than the average inmate.* He took out a syringe Sam gave him in the car. It was already full of heroin. He lowered his pants and sat on the toilet. Feeling the cold pain in his thigh, he inhaled, waiting for the warmth to overtake him. Ted sat there for a moment before getting up and using the toilet. He flushed, washed his hands, and looked again in the mirror. Still, the circles remained. Still, the beard needed trimming. He picked up his razor and examined the blades. *I could use these blades to do it.* He shook his head. *No, it would be too messy. Maybe I should trim my beard now.* He set the razor down. *No, then it won't look like me.* He looked at himself again. *Then again, my parents will probably have it cut. I need to write it into my will, my letter, my whatever that no one can cut my beard.* He opened the door and sat on the living room couch. Falling over, he let the euphoria overtake him as he lay on the plush couch.

He did not hear Chris ring the bell.

Allison stopped. This was unexpected. Adia had dyed her hair again. It was black with red streaks. *I just want a beer and I get an ex. What the heck?* She stood there amid the streetlights, shirt waving with the breeze.

Adia was ten feet from her in a red sundress and black flats. Her beaded hemp necklace shone in the night. She laughed. "I figured I would see you eventually." She walked over to Allison.

Allison backed up a few feet and narrowed her eyes. "Why are you here?"

"Shh…don't say anything." Adia grabbed her wrist and pulled her close.

Allison caught the scent of patchouli and her body awakened out of habit. She let herself feel the kiss through every nerve. There they stood for what seemed like minutes. With the sound of a passing car, she returned to the moment. "Wha…What are you doing?" Allison jerked away.

"I'm just saying 'Hello.'" Adia smiled, lip gloss shining with the moonlight.

"What's going on?" Allison took a few more steps back. "I…I have to go home now." She turned to leave.

"No you don't. Luke told me you were meeting him tonight." Adia shrugged at the building and leaned against the exterior. She cocked her head toward Allison. "You don't want to disappoint him, do you? It might be detrimental to your 'art' career."

Allison winced as she finger quoted the word 'art.' "Ugh, fine. Why do you need to be here anyway?"

Adia got off the wall and pointed to the second story window. "I live there." She grinned. "So I'll be seeing you around." She opened the red wooden door, sending a few paint chips to the ground.

Allison paused for a moment before entering the bar. *Great. Now I have to deal with her.* She saw Luke's smiling face and ordered a Jack and Coke.

"Double, Luke."

"Bad day?"

"Yeah."

She stayed there for about an hour before leaving. She opened the door and Adia was still there.

There was something about her. The way that she stood there with the city behind her, before entering her apartment. Intimacy was never this intimate. Green tinted smoke disappeared into the night sky as Adia stood before her. Just like before. Allison inhaled the earthy smell and closed her eyes, imagining the satin sheets beneath them.

"Something the matter, baby?" Adia put the roach away and stroked Allison's hoodie, knocking her out of her trance.

"N…Nothing." She crossed her arms.

"Yeah right. I know that face." Adia pulled her into the doorway. "Come up. I have something to show you."

"What could you possibly have to show me?" Allison hesitated and Susan flashed in her mind.

"It's a surprise." She ascended the creaky stairs. "You'll love it."

Allison ran her hand over the wooden doorframe. *What do I do?* She caught another whiff of Adia's perfume. She groaned. *I haven't had any in a long time.* She glanced back outside at the passing cars as Susan flashed again in her mind. *She's totally not gay…Or at least she says she's not.*

"Come on, Allison!" Adia beckoned as she unlocked her apartment.

Allison put one foot in front of the other. Her body screamed for the patchouli-scented hair, the soft caresses, the liberation. *It's just sex, right?* She closed her eyes for a second and entered the apartment.

It was just like before. Throw pillows were

166

strewn about the couches and floor. It was a Bohemian's dream. Rich reds and golds embellished the ancient walls and decrepit linoleum. Adia was flitting about, lighting candles and incense.

"I have some DVDs if you'd like to watch something." She lit another wick.

"Naw." Allison sat down on the couch. *It's just sex. No emotions. No anything. Just sex.* There was a pang in her stomach. *Susan wouldn't like this.* Another pang. *Susan doesn't need to know.* "I don't want to watch a movie."

Adia turned around and approached her. "Allison, I've missed you." She inched closer and flicked her hair, causing it to fall over her eyes. She sat down on the couch, sinking in a few inches, and traced a line with her finger from Allison's knee to her thigh. "I've missed *you.*"

Allison shifted toward her. *It's just sex.* She looked into never ending brown eyes. "I've missed having *you.*" Allison grazed Adia's thigh with her fingertip.

"We need to remedy that." Adia whispered into her ear with a slight nibble to the lobe. She led a trail of kisses down her neck and back up to her mouth. "Unnn...I've missed your cherry lips." She breathed and slid her hand under Allison's shirt. She kissed her again as she straddled her.

Allison leaned back so that Adia covered her whole body. Adia unhooked her bra from the outside and pulled the shirt over her head, causing it to fall upon Allison.

Adia took the bra and tossed it across the room. "I've missed your scent, your everything."

Allison drew her closer. "Show me how much you've missed me."

Adia ripped Allison's shirt off and nibbled around her bra. "You don't need that." She reached under her and removed Allison's bra, exposing her breasts to the incense infused air.

Allison lay ready for the other woman's tongue exploration, as it got warmer and warmer in the apartment. Soon both women were entangled amid wisps of smoke and soft lighting. Adia made her way downward and Allison lost herself.

Daylight came and Allison woke first. She rushed to get dressed and left without Adia noticing. *What have I done? How could I be so foolish?* She got into her car and cried to the sound of Sarah McLachlan. She slammed her hand on the steering wheel. *How could I have done this to Susan?* She sobbed louder. *Why is Susan*

straight? I love her. Why can't I be with her?
What is wrong with me? She stopped sobbing
long enough to start the car and drive home.
There is no way that I will be able to work today.
No way to create. I only want to destroy.

Twenty-Seven

Ted finished a bottle of Jack and threw it across the room. He leaned back on the bed and felt the rush of alcohol through his veins. His vision blurred and he thought of Susan, of Sam, of life, of Livi with flowers in her wavy hair.

"Could you have it any other way, Livi?" He put his fingers up to the ceiling and spread them apart, watching the memories flowing through them. They floated like dust caught in the wind. Like life adrift in the ocean of time.

There, Livi was staring at his bed. Staring at him. Staring at his soul.

"I'm sorry," he whispered.

Her vacant eyes stared past him. The petals began to float to the ground and then the ceiling. She turned around and showed him the back of her head. She touched her matted hair. "Look what you did, Teddy, look what you did." She put her hands to her face and sobbed.

"I'm sorry," he sobbed louder. "I'm sorry!" He grimaced and covered his eyes with his arm, feeling the wetness of his tears.

"There's no excuse." She stopped sobbing

and composed herself. "You should feel what I felt."

He blinked and she was gone.

"If only for a night, I could forget it." Ted took out his stash from his nightstand and removed a syringe. He twirled it for a moment, prepping himself for the familiar sting. He stuck it into his thigh and the liquid disappeared into his veins.

Colors blurred.

He felt himself rise.

Livi gave him half of a grilled cheese sandwich and a glass of Kool-Aid.

Susan sent a smile in his direction.

Sam lay next to him with those lips.

Those lips.

Rain fell in puddles.

There was a funeral.

A road trip.

Love.

Darkness.

Twenty-Eight

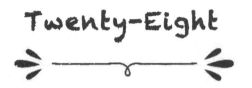

Susan knocked on Ted's door. Silence. She knocked again. Still nothing. Trembling, she burst into the bedroom. *Thank God, we're best friends!* She saw him on the bed. At first, she did nothing. He looked like he was sleeping. Susan noticed that the window was left open and rain was drenching the carpet. She walked over and shut it. That's when she noticed the syringe on the mattress. Her eyes widened and she rushed to check his pulse. He was cold, but there was still life. She grabbed his phone and dropped it. She picked it up, heart pounding and punched 911. She ran to unlock the front door and ran back to Ted.

She held his hand and prayed to whatever deity was watching until the paramedics showed up. They pushed her to the side. She crossed her arms and trembled as she watched them try to revive him, failing at first. They loaded him onto a stretcher and took him away.

She ran to get her keys, knocked a piece of paper off the nightstand. *Huh?* It was a letter. She unfolded it. She put her hands to her lips as

172

she read. *This is not happening. No. No. No.*
Fumbling with her ignition, she sped to the hospital.

Susan sat and listened to the heart monitor.
The staccato beeped with her pulse as she
watched her friend sacrifice himself to the technological monster surrounding his bed. Ted's labored breaths complemented the imposing sea
green wallpaper. She leaned forward on her elbow, chin nestled in her palm. She tapped her
upper lip to the music of the hospital room. Her
fingers drumming to the somber cadence as she
sat.

"Where's his family?" she asked the silence.

There was a tap on the door. Expecting a
nurse, she straightened her posture. She slumped
again when she realized that it was just Sam.

"Hey, Susan," Sam droned as she sat down
some plastic bags on the end table.

*Why the fuck is she here? She doesn't deserve to be here, with him. She fucked him up.
This is her own damn fault.* "Uh, hi, Sam." Susan
clenched her teeth watched as Sam stumbled.
Then she noticed the shaking. "Are you okay?"
She feigned concern.

"I'm fine. Having a boyfriend attempt suicide is common relationship milestone." Sam rolled her eyes behind her sunglasses.

"I don't need the sarcasm right now." Susan rolled her eyes. *She's such a goddamn bitch.*

"Whatever." Sam sat opposite her.

"Look, we're both adults and dealing with shit right now." Susan tried to control herself and calm herself down.

"Yeah." She stared at her boyfriend who drifted in and out of consciousness. "Overdose?"

"Yeah." Susan crossed her legs. *Obviously.*

"I love him, you know."

"Honestly, it's kinda hard to tell." Susan sucked her teeth.

"What do you mean?" Sam's brow furrowed.

"I mean, he *never* did any drugs, other than weed, before he met you." Her tear soaked eyes met Sam's. She was trembling, now.

"Are you saying that this is my fault?"

"Not directly." Susan could feel Sam's glare through the sunglasses. "I mean, I think, the drugs caused this and that you *could* have stopped him." She checked her phone, trying to calm herself. *I can't see her right now.* "I will let you guys have some alone time." She gathered her things and left.

Twenty-Nine

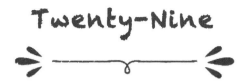

Ted stared at the wall. Visitation hours were over and nothing was on TV. He sighed and looked at his IV. Fluid traveled from the bag into his veins as the machine beeped a staccato rhythm. He listened, mesmerized, for an hour. Then darkness fell and he was whisked away to fog.

"You failed." Livi smiled as she threw pink flower petals in the air. He stood there and stared at her. She twirled to face him. Laughing again, she tossed some petals in his direction. "I should have known. Ha! Ha! You've always failed. Failed. Failed at everything." Her face twisted into a grimace and she laughed louder.

Ted was twelve again as she disappeared. It was no longer dark and foggy, but sunny and warm. The green grass complemented the white casket as the priest sprinkled holy water on the lacquered cedar.

"It is time to rest, Livi." The priest mono-toned as the casket was lowered into a foggy pit.

Ted stared at the casket until it disappeared

into the darkness, surrounded by gray plumes. Everyone disappeared and he crept to the unfilled grave. He peered into the foggy flames. There was no casket, just a body. It lay there motionless, neither male nor female. He looked at his hands; he aged ten years. Ted stepped back as he watched the body float into the air. A loud roar erupted and he was knocked down.

He couldn't take his eyes off the corpse as it spoke. "I am nothing and everything and everyone and something. I am you. I am Livi. I am life. I am death. We are all connected. Your death was life. Her life was death."

It dissipated into smoke and he woke in a sweat.

What the fuck?

Thirty

Susan sat in the overstuffed armchair and sipped on a cup of store brand coffee. The blandness was masked by her sadness. Ted was in the hospital and Allison wasn't hers and never would be. *I'm such a pansy. I should call her.* She stared at the phone on the end table. *I can't. Ted said that he did this to free us. How so? I don't get it.* She reread the letter.

She brought her thumb and forefinger to her nose bridge. *Why? Ugh.* She removed her hand from her face and looked through the window. *I almost lost my best friend. Damn it. God damn it.* She brought her hand back up to her forehead. *Life is too short for this bullshit. But my life is worthless without him or Allison. What do I do? What the* fuck *do I do? I need to talk to her. I need to tell her. I need to love her.*

She got up to dump her coffee. *She should be working now. I should tell her* now. *I need better coffee anyway.* She went to her bedroom and put on her most flattering jeans and layered a blue plaid shirt over a form fitting, black tank top. She laced up her sneakers and left with a slight slam of the door. She rushed to her car so fast that she forgot to release the emergency brake until she was halfway down the block.

"Damn it!' she cursed aloud. *I'm going to tell her today. I can do this. Life's too short not to. I need to come out. I need to be with her.* She got to the coffee shop and Allison wasn't there.

"She called in sick." Chris wiped up some vagabond sugar. "Said she had a stomach ache or something."

I hope she's okay. Susan set to work. *I should stop by after work and see her. Maybe bring her some medicine. She'd like that.*

Then Allison walked into the store.

"I thought you were sick, Allie," Susan called with a smile.

"I…I am…kinda." Allison put on an apron. "I just…I just had a rough night. I was going to stay home, but I can't afford it."

Her eyes are puffy. Susan grabbed her arm. "Hey, if you need to talk. I'm here."

Allison avoided her gaze. "I don't know, Susan." She escaped her grasp. "I just don't know."

Susan felt the familiar doubt rise up in her stomach. *Maybe I upset her? What did I do?*

Chris went into his office and gestured toward Allison. She closed the door behind them. Susan could only make out soft, curt whispers.

"I can't," she thought she heard Allison cry.

Her heart sank.

The door chimed and Susan fumbled with the next five orders before Allison emerged, eyes less puffy, but still red. She did not say a word to Susan the rest of the shift and left as soon as her shift was over.

What the fuck did I do? Susan drove to the bar after closing. Maybe Luke can explain what's going on. She parked her car and watched as Allison was greeted by a woman with dark hair and bangles.

They kissed.

Susan sank.

Thirty-One

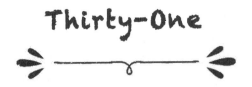

Allison sat on the couch, stroking her cat as she thought of her next art piece. *I need to push the boundaries further. Maybe do something more graphic?* She shook her head. *That would end badly.* Her eyes wandered to the Ani Di-Franco poster on the opposite wall. She sat up. The cat leapt and hissed. *Ani wouldn't care, why should I?* She paced across the carpet, causing the oak floorboards underneath to hem and haw. *Hmm...What should I do?* She looked back at the poster. *Feminism. I must include feminism.* She looked from her art supplies to her couch to the newspaper. Allison picked it up from the coffee table. "Omaha Woman 'Asked for It.'" She read the article. "That's idiotic!" She said aloud to herself. "No woman ever asks to be raped." Throwing the paper down in anger, she looked at her art supplies again. *I need to do something related to this. This. This is going to be big.*

Allison turned on her stereo and blasted Sleater-Kinney as she drew a rudimentary stencil of a woman on cardboard. It was an outline of a woman lying on her back with an exaggerated

180

vulva. Above the woman, she carved out the words "Still not asking for it" in capital letters. She grinned at her handiwork. *I should spray paint this is several places.* She sat cross-legged and tapped her chin. *Hmm... I've already done UNO, so they've probably upped their security. I need somewhere downtown, somewhere in Dundee, Benson, and West Omaha. The West Omaha piece has to be the biggest. I need to teach those pretentious white men something.* She looked at the time. 11:00. She had time to do this tonight.

She gathered her paint and stencils and got dressed. It was a somewhat warm night with just a touch of coldness brought in by the wind. *It's obvious that I should do the downtown piece first as the police aren't patrolling heavily because the bars aren't closed yet. Then I will hit up Benson and Dundee. West Omaha will be last, because they don't have as much crime. Gotta avoid the cops!* She laughed to herself.

Allison spotted a large billboard advertising a major bank situated on top of a closed sandwich shop. *Perfect.* She pulled on her ski mask and climbed the fire exit onto the roof. In a matter of seconds, she had done her first stencil. *No time to admire, I gotta be quick.* She half jumped, half climbed down and roared off in her car. *I feel like Thelma and Louise.*

Benson was easy. She spray-painted a gas

station at the corner of 50th and Maple that had damaged streetlights. Dundee was a bit more difficult as the main street was populated with scores of hipsters enjoying the nice night. *I have to be quick again.* She scowled at the populace. *Ugh.* She surveyed the area again and found a nice shadowy area on the side of the Dundee Theater. *Hmm...It's not too visible, but not too bad. It'll have to do.* She rushed out of her car, sprayed, and ran back in under five minutes. Allison breathed a sigh of relief as she sped down Dodge. *That was harrowing.* She checked herself out in the mirror after she removed her mask. *I feel awesome, though. One more stop.*

She drove out to Oak View Mall and sat in an adjacent parking lot while she took note of the security. *They drive by about every fifteen minutes. I'm going to do the main entrance. But, there are cameras. Hmm... Duct tape.* She found a dark place and covered her license plates with tape. After the security did their rounds, she drove up and spray painted her stencil right by the main entrance. *People will definitely see this.* She grinned, got back in her car, and drove back to her hideaway to remove the tape. After she was done, she cruised back to her apartment, undressed, and fell asleep.

The social media was once again buzzing with pomp and controversy. Allison lay in bed and scrolled through her phone. One of her friends had posted a picture of the Benson piece and attracted several conflicting comments. "What idiocy! No one has respect for public property anymore!" "What genius! Truly an example of modern feminism!"

She felt excitement take over as she rolled out of bed and felt the oak under her bare feet. *So cold!* She looked out the window. *Rain? I was hoping for sunshine. Oh, well.* She sighed and walked to her kitchen. She found a bag of dark roasted coffee sitting on the counter. *I don't remember putting that there.* She picked it up and turned it over. There was a yellow note stuck to the orange foil.

"I know it's you" was written in block letters.

Fear replaced excitement as she grabbed a steak knife from the drawer by the sink. She tiptoed out of the kitchen and into the living area. Something stirred on the couch under a fleece blanket. Allison approached the lump, knife drawn. She grabbed the blanket and threw it across the room. There was the intruder. There was Chris.

"Are you insane?!" she shouted as she punched him in the stomach only to invoke laughter from the offending party. She dropped the knife.

Still laughing, Chris sat up. "You should know better than to leave your door unlocked at night."

"I must have spaced out last night." She walked back to the kitchen. "Was it you who left this bag of coffee on the counter?"

"You betcha."

"That was really creepy and not funny."

"It was funny to me." Chris laughed again as he put his hand to his forehead.

Allison rolled her eyes and started a pot of coffee. "Why aren't you at work?"

"I took a personal day. Susan's opening for me." Chris watched her put the coffee bag in the cupboard. "Go ahead and go in two hours later. I'm pretty sure we're going to be slow today anyway."

Allison cocked her eyebrow. "Why's that?"

"It's the weekend. Duh."

"Oh, right." Allison savored the rich vapors as she poured two cups of coffee. *If Chris is an expert on anything legal, it's picking out coffee.*

"So you hear about the 'vandalism' last night?" Chris finger quoted.

"I saw something about it on Facebook." Allison sat down.

"I wonder who's doing it." He smirked and looked out the window.

"I don't know." *Thank goodness, he's not*

looking at me. She sipped her coffee. "Why are you here annoying me this morning?"

"I wanted to discuss the street art with you." He sipped his coffee and closed his eyes. "Mmmm…Man, that's good stuff." He set the cup down on the coffee table with a slight click.

I hope he doesn't suspect me. Allison shifted in her seat. *Maybe he saw me last night. But he smokes every night and doesn't normally leave his house afterwards.* "Oh?"

"Yeah. They showed pictures on the news of a car at Oakview Mall." He smiled. "It looks *very* similar to yours."

"But I stayed in last night."

Chris tilted his head. "Really? Because I think it's *very* unlikely that someone else has a dent on the driver's side of the hood *and* a floral decal on the back window *and* an Ani DiFranco bumper sticker."

Darn it! I need to cover up those stickers! Allison took a shaky sip of her coffee.

Chris chuckled. "You've never been a good liar."

"I'm going to take those stickers off my car."

"I've already done it. I didn't want to blow my sister's cover."

"Did you write that creepy note?"

"Yep! Ha ha!" He leaned forward and clasped his hands between his knees. "I love

185

your work and I want to say that it'll start a *revolution* in Omaha. I also want to say that we should use it to gain publicity for the shop."

His business tone is not much different than his joke tone. Mer. Allison cocked her brow again. "How so?"

"I want Omaha's Banksy to make an appearance."

Allison sat her cup down and glanced out the window. *Might as well.* She met her brother's eyes. "Fine. I will do it."

Chris grinned from ear to ear. "Sweet!"

Her work was all the buzz on the radio as well. In addition to her car, they even got some good pictures of her in her ninja garb. Allison smiled as she checked her Facebook again. Everyone was talking about her, and her conservative acquaintances were furious. She chuckled as the broadcasters censored her artwork and called her the "Banksy of the Midwest." She got dressed in jeans and a plaid shirt. Before leaving for work, she put her hair up and tied a bandana around her head. *I totally feel like Rosie today.*

She smiled as she entered Cool Beans. She saw that Susan looked sullen and her high fell. *She's. Not. Gay.*

Thirty-Two

"I hate that coffee always makes me thirsty." Susan put away her empty cup when there was a break in the customer flow. "I'm always following it up with pop or water."

"I know, right?" Allison said as she put her dishrag away.

"I'm going to have a pop." Susan opened the employee mini fridge.

Allison grabbed her hand. "Pop's bad for you; have water instead."

Susan shot a glance at Allison. "So's deception."

"What's up with you today?" Allison backed up a few inches.

"Nothing."

Allison clicked her teeth. "You just said deception's bad for you. I know when you're lying."

"Yes, I'm a hypocrite. I know." Susan turned her back toward her. *Should I tell her what I saw that night?* Susan took a sip of her pop. *I should. I'm also going to say that I'm on my period. Yeah, that's a good excuse for my bitchiness to-*

day. I'm probably not her type, anyway. She sighed. "Sorry, Allie. I'm just starting my period."

"It's ok." Allison cleaned the counter.

"So, have a hot date the other night?" Susan leaned against the opposite corner.

"What do you mean?" Allison stopped cleaning and turned around.

"I saw you the other night outside the bar with some girl."

Allison resumed cleaning. "Oh, her? She's just a past fling who wanted to meet up."

"It looked like you guys did have history."

"We did." Allison turned around again and sighed.

It looks like she is about to cry. "Wanna get drinks after work and talk about it?"

Allison looked straight into Susan's eyes. "Yes."

The door chimed and Susan said, "Welcome!" with a smile. *She looks familiar.*

"Adia?!" Allison stood rigid in front of the cash register.

Adia was wearing a free flowing red Bohemian style sundress with simple red sandals. She took off her sunglasses and leaned against the counter. She chewed on her frames as she met the cashier's eyes. "Hey, babe, I heard you worked here." She trailed her finger along the edge of the glass case. "I would like to taste your..." she rested her finger, "coffee." She smiled. Adia turned her attention to Susan, "What's good here?"

"Uh...Um... The iced mocha's pretty good. Especially on a hot day like this." She fidgeted with her apron.

"Yeah, I'll have that." Adia examined Allison. "The eye candy here makes up for the poor service." She laughed.

It's her. Allison's ex. Seeing her coworker's shock, Susan took Adia's money and made her coffee.

"Thanks, honey." She smiled at Susan and turned to Allison. "I'll be seeing you later." She laughed and sauntered out of the coffee shop.

"That was awkward." Susan cleaned the coffee machine.

"Yeah." Allison lowered her head.

"She seemed like a creep." *If that's my competition, maybe I have a chance. I mean, Allison didn't seem to like that she showed up. But still, it* did *seem like she enjoyed kissing her the other night. Ugh. I have to tell her how I feel.*

"Yeah." Allison went back to work as several customers came into the store. "I'll tell you the rest after work."

The bar was low key and unfamiliar, but welcoming. The golden brown light added a comforting aura that begged the two women to stay. They brush passed some jocks and got a couple of microbrews from the middle-aged bartender. After they found a vinyl booth tucked away in the corner, Susan slid in after Allison. *Allison looks pretty shaken. I don't think I like that Adia chick. She seems like a bitch.*

"What's up, Allie?" Susan crossed her feet underneath the table. "That Adia chick gave me bad vibes."

"I don't like her." Allison looked past her.

"Obviously." Susan pointed her eyes. "What did she do?" Susan watched as Allison's eyes grew distant for a moment then snapped back to reality. *She looked like Ted just now. Shit. I really don't like this Adia chick.*

Allison sighed. "She made me fall in love with her. She seemed like the best thing ever. Then after we had dated a few months, she changed. She became mean and controlling." Allison took a long drink from her beer. "She caused me to fail out of college. She thought I spent too much time on my artwork." She slammed her beer down.

190

Susan looked at the table and breathed inward. "I knew there was something off about her." She paused and felt an ache in her chest. "I'm glad...I'm glad you're not with her anymore."

Allison played with her napkin. "Me too." She released the crushed paper. "At least I was until she showed up in Omaha. Now she scares me."

"Why is she here? Is she that dangerous?"

"I wouldn't say 'dangerous,' but she is unstable. Apparently she wants to get back together."

Susan took a drink of her beer and let her lips linger on the bottle before she sat it down. Her chest lurched. "Do you?"

"No way!" Susan's chest relaxed as Allison continued. "Absolutely not!" She paused again. "I found out after we broke up that she stalked a couple of her exes."

I definitely don't like her now. Susan took another swig of beer and looked Allison straight in the eye. "If you need anything, I'm only a text away." She grabbed her hand and Allison surrendered to her touch.

"Thank you." Allison glanced at the bar. "I'm going to get us more beer. Just one more round." She gave a half smile. "I don't want to be hung over tomorrow." She left with a flick of her hair.

Susan watched her every step and played with her empty bottle. *I've got it bad. I just want to hold her and kiss her problems away. I wonder what she's doing after this. Maybe I could invite her over to watch a movie.*

Allison returned with their beer. "Some dude bought these for us."

"Score!" Susan reached for her beer. She drew circles in the condensation on the table as she asked, "Would you like to come over and watch a movie?"

"Sure."

Allison sat on Susan's couch as the other woman grabbed some pop from the kitchen. *I wonder if she feels sorry for me. I hope she doesn't, but I bet she does.* She watched Susan bend down. Her jean pockets added to the curvature of her body. *Mmmm...I wish she were gay.* She drew a throw pillow close as she watched her breasts sway with every step.

"I hope you like Coke, Allie. Even if it's bad for you." Susan chuckled.

"Anything is fine right now, jerk." She smiled. She looked around the living room.

"Isn't Ted normally around?"

"Lately, he's been spending time with Sam." Susan sighed. "He randomly went to Denver."

"Why?" *She looks really concerned.*

"I don't know. He's been acting weird lately. I bet Sam got him high and convinced him to go." She went over to the DVDs and sighed again. "You know, Allison, I really don't feel like a movie anymore."

"Do you want me to leave?" *Did I do something wrong?*

"No. I just want to chill." Susan sat down beside Allison. Her arm brushed Allison's leg and goosebumps formed on her arm.

I want to cuddle. But she's not gay. Allison inched away.

Susan put her hand on her thigh. "Allie, I want you to be safe."

Allison met her gaze. *I want to kiss her so badly.* "I am safe, here with you." Allison choked back her feelings.

Susan moved in closer. *This is torture. Pure unadulterated torture. I just want her lips, her everything.* She felt a tug on her chin and a softness on her lips. Closing her eyes, she imagined how she'd taste. *She said she wasn't gay!* Allison broke the kiss.

"You said you weren't gay." *How could she play a cruel joke like this? I felt safe!*

193

Susan stroked Allison's hand. "I like you, Allie, more than a straight girl should." She backed away. "I'm gay, Allie. I'm gay."

Allison pulled Susan in closer. "I know." She kissed her again. Her head was filled with memories. Memories of Kansas City. Memories of her. Memories of Adia. She started to cry. "But, I can't be with you yet."

Susan saw her tears and understood. She put her arms around the other woman and drew her to her breast. "I'm here if you need me. Fuck Adia."

Thirty-Three

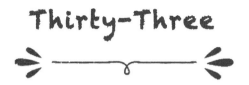

Susan came down the stairs to open the door. *I don't know why he can't just text me. I have chores to do.* She half flung the door open. "Hi, Chris. You want a beer?"

"Naw, I'm good."

Susan closed the door as she stepped outside on the porch. "So what's this big announcement you have?"

"Well," he sat in on of the chairs and lit up a joint, "I was going to save this for work tomorrow, but I've already told Allie, so I might as well tell you in advance." He grinned. "I'm so excited to tell you that we're having that ninja street artist make an appearance on Wednesday."

Susan narrowed her eyes. "Why Wednesday?"

"Because most people will have plans on Friday." He rolled his eyes. "Plus, that's the only time I was able to schedule a press conference." He offered the joint to Susan.

Should I? Fuck it; it's been a rough week. Susan hesitated before taking it and took a long drag. She exhaled. "A press conference?"

"Yeah. All the news people want to find out who this vigilante is and I've promised them that I would have her at my shop."

"It's a woman?"

"Yeah."

"Did you meet her?" *What the fuck does he do in his spare time when he doesn't smoke?*

"Yeah." He took another puff before passing it back to Susan. "I randomly walked in on her working in an alley. I recognized her from those pictures on Facebook."

That doesn't seem believable at all, but do I really want to know how he knows her? Susan let Chris continue.

"Anyway, so I'm like, 'I like your work, do you like coffee?' She was like, 'Yeah.'" He grinned. "So I'm like, 'Wanna make an appearance at my coffee shop? It'd be good exposure and I'd pay you well.' She thought about it and agreed. We exchanged numbers. Badda bing. Badda boom." Chris flashed his palms in a flamboyant gesture. "That's how we booked the hottest local artist of this year." He finished his joint. "We're about to be the most famous coffee shop around."

Susan rolled her eyes at his absurdity, but felt a kick inside. "Hell yeah! This is going to be awesome!" *Maybe I can learn something from this woman. Maybe she can teach me to be strong.*

Chris stood up and looked at his phone. "It's about that time. I gotta jet." He descended the steps. "I'll see you bright and early tomorrow morning!"

Susan shook her head as he left then went back inside to her bedroom. She sat on the multi-colored afghan and stared out the window. The sky was darkening and rain soon poured out in buckets. She found herself back in her mother's kitchen.

It was the eve of her high school graduation. Gifts of teddy bears and money littered her end table and she stared at her ceiling. I can't believe this is really happening. I'm graduating high school! I'm going to be free of this town! It's going to be awesome! *She thought of her best friend, Ashley. Long brown hair and a smile as bright as stars.* I'm going to call her. *She got up out of bed and went downstairs to their landline. Her parents were out at her aunt's, prepping for her party tomorrow. They wouldn't be back until late.*

"Hey, Ashley, wanna come over?" Susan twisted the phone cord in her fingers.

"Sure." came the mellow voice.

Susan hurried to tidy her room. She found some DVDs to watch. Ten minutes passed and the doorbell rang.

"Hey, girl!" Susan greeted her friend as she let her into the living room. "Wanna watch some DVDs?"

"Alright, but can we watch it in your room?" Ashley set down her purse. Her low-rise jeans exposed the hem of her blue, lace panties. She was already heading to the stairs.

"Okay. I'm going to make some popcorn first." She went into the kitchen.

Once in her room, Susan popped in a teenage comedy and they lay on her afghan. They watched the movie for the better part of an hour before deeming it too stupid and turning it off.

Ashley sat up and ran her finger along the afghan's yarn. "You know, I'm kinda nervous about tomorrow, Susie."

"I'm not. I'm excited to leave this town." Susan also sat up and leaned against her headboard.

"Yeah. I am too, but I will miss you." Ashley looked like she was about to cry.

"Don't cry! We'll still have Facebook and we'll keep in touch!"

"I'm not going to cry." Ashley scooted closer. "And I know we'll keep in touch. It's just...It's just...I have to do something before we leave."

"What's that?" Susan put the half empty

popcorn bowl on the end table.

Ashley leaned in and lifted the other girl's face. Their lips met and Susan's eyes widened. What is this? I'm not gay. Am I? No, but this feels nice. *Susan let Ashley's hands explore her body and she felt yearning for the first time. Nothing she had experienced in her youth felt this good.*

Ashley and Susan spent a few hours tasting and touching each other until they were exhausted. Ashley held Susan in her arms. "Susan," her voice trembled, "We can't tell anyone about this."

"Yeah."

"Just so you know, I'm not gay, I just love you."

"Yeah. Neither am I." They both giggled.

Thirty-Four

The shop was teeming with beards and plaid as Allie stood in the supply closet and covered her face with a pink bandana and sunglasses. She caught her reflection in some broken coffee mugs. *I'm a carbon copy of Banksy.* She shook her head. *Next time, I need to do something original.* She put on some gloves and slid out the door. She ran into Chris.

"Cigarette break?" She leaned against the brick.

"No. Just taking a quick hit." He put his lighter into his shirt pocket. "Oh, I have something for you." He took something rectangular out of the brown knapsack by his Toms. "It's a voice distorter. Put it on."

"You know, for a stoner, you're a genius." Allie took the object from her brother.

"It's the weed." Chris stood lookout while Allie undid her get up and adjusted the distorter so it was fastened under the hoodie and around her ear. He gave her a once over. "Sweet! Let's get this show on the road." He opened the door and motioned for her to follow.

Their feet clacked on the cracked, brown tile as they made their way from the back door to the counter. Susan was focused on pouring and mixing, her movements in sync with the crowd and the acoustic background music. *She flows like water.* Allison watched her for a moment. *I wonder how she is in bed.* Allison's eyes widened behind her glasses. *No, I can't focus on her right now.* She turned her head to the crowd milled about before her. *Artists. Writers. Musicians. Even reporters! This is great!* She scanned the crowd again and stopped at a woman in the corner. *I should have known she'd be here.* Adia was leaning against the flier-covered bulletin board, an ironic scarf dangling around her neck and shoulders. *That's weird. Is she trying to fit in?*

Allison followed Chris to the stage. *She must not want me to know she's here.* Her chair creaked as she sat down behind a table in the center. Her brother adjusted the microphone as he settled down beside her. One by one, the crowd began to take notice and quiet down. Chris smiled. His shaggy dreaded hair fell in his face as he turned to Allison and back to the crowd.

"Hi, everyone! I'm glad you could make it to this press conference of sorts. I'm hoping that you're enjoying coffee as we speak. Susan over there," he gestured toward the counter. "is one of my top baristas. She's so good, she can make dog coffee fresh again." He smiled again. "Let's give it up for her!"

A rush of applause broke out and Allison watched Susan smile as several customers approached the counter. She turned her attention back to Chris as he continued.

"So, we have the legend herself here in our midst." Another round of applause. "She's here to answer any and all questions you have."

"Are you single?" came a male voice in the back. It was met with laughter.

Allison shifted. "No comment."

"Aw, c'mon!" said the same voice. "Don't you want to come home with me?" He laughed and turned to his friend, spilling his drink.

Allison tapped her fingers and sucked her teeth. Chris moved the mic towards himself. "Please refrain from catcalling our guest." The women in the room cheered and Allison relaxed.

The reporters scribbled something on their notepads. One of them lifted her pen. "Why do you disguise yourself?"

Allison took the mic. "Well, I don't want to be caught 'vandalizing' property."

The reporter followed with, "Do you really think your work is vandalism?"

"No, it's a public service."

Another reporter interjected. "But you're defacing public buildings. How is *that* a public service?"

Allison clasped her hands on top of the table and leaned toward the crowd. "Well, as you can see by the remark from the man in the back, we need to create a safer space for women, a safer space for everyone. How is that NOT a public service?"

The crowd cheered. Another reporter asked, "Is it really worth it to cause these businesses to spend hundreds of dollars to clean up your graffiti?"

"It's not graffiti. It's art."

"How is it art?"

"It evokes emotions." Allison shook her head.

The male reporter tapped his chin with his pen. "What type of emotion are you trying to evoke?"

"Anger."

"Why?"

"Because I'm angry that there are people who are treated as less than human."

"This is the twenty-first century, it's not that big of a problem."

Allison felt rage well up inside her and she pointed at him. "You're a man. You don't know what it's like being a woman."

"Women have it good now. Besides, *not all men* treat women differently." He was met with silence from the crowd.

Allison straightened her posture. "You're wrong. Women, especially queer women and women of color, are still discriminated against in the professional and personal world. We need to change this. We need to change Omaha." She paused. "We need to change the world." The crowd cheered.

This time, a woman in plaid raised her hand. Allison noticed remnants of acrylic paint on her shirt. "Are you paying homage to Banksy? Do you feel street art really has a place in Omaha?"

"In a roundabout way, I guess I am paying homage to Banksy. He does have a way of stirring controversy, but I like to keep my work original." She looked around the room. "As far as whether street art has a place in Omaha, I think it has a place everywhere. It should not be limited to tagging in ganglands. It's a voice from the inner city. It's a cry for help. It's hope. It's everything art *is* and *should* be."

"Aren't you afraid the police will find out who you are?"

"If they do, I'd do my time. Arrests have a way of moving people. Look at Pussy Riot. Arrests are an art form of their own." She smiled. "*Besides*, I think the police have their hands full trying to keep guns off the street. As it should be. They shouldn't give their valuable time to catching a *non-violent* artist."

"Hell, fuck yeah!" shouted a woman.

Allison smiled behind her bandana, her mouth's precipitation moistening her lips. She checked the time. Adia was now standing by a bookshelf, grinning. *Fuck me. She probably knows who I am. I must cut this short.* "Hey, Chris, I thank you for having me tonight. I gotta jet."

Chris nodded. "I'm so glad you could make it today!" He smiled at the crowd. "Let's give it up for our ninja!"

Allison left the stage amid applause and camera flashes. She ran through the crowd and out the back door. She ripped off her outfit in the back alley and stored her clothes behind the dumpster for safekeeping. Jogging to the corner, she fixed her hair into a ponytail and sauntered through the shop's front door. She cut through the people, ignoring Adia, and met Susan at the counter. "Oh, man, I missed her, didn't I?"

"Yeah, it was awesome." Susan handed out a mocha. "You can still help, though." She half-smiled, light reflecting off her hair.

Allison's nerves jolted. "I love you... I mean. 'alright.'" *Ugh. What did I do?*

Susan dropped the saucer she was holding

with a loud crash. "What?"

"Nothing." Allison bent over and started to clean up the mess.

"Yeah, what?" Adia stood by the counter with her arms crossed. She stared into Allison's eyes.

Allison stood straight up. "This doesn't concern you, Adia."

"Yes it does." Fire welled in her face. "Anything that involves you involves me. I'm your true love."

Susan approached Adia. "I'm pretty sure you're not. Now if you would kindly leave the store."

"No."

"I'm sorry, did I stutter?" Susan raised her eyebrows.

Adia swung at Susan and missed. A small crowd gathered around. Chris interrupted the conversation he was having in the corner to make his way over to the women. "What's going on?"

Allison took a step toward him. "Adia tried to hit Susan."

Chris turned to Adia. "Are you stupid? Do you not see Susan's muscles? She could take you. Now leave the damn store."

Adia threw her arms in the air. "What are you going to do? Call the cops?"

"If I have to."

"Fine." Adia turned to leave. "You better watch your back, Susan. She belongs to me, bitch."

"She's fucking crazy." Susan dumped the broken dish in the trash as the crowd watched her leave.

"Yeah, she kinda is." Chris stepped behind the counter to help the next person in line.

Susan turned to Allison. "Allie, come over tonight. Please."

Should I? Allison looked into Susan's face. Her eyes trembled. "Okay."

Thirty-Five

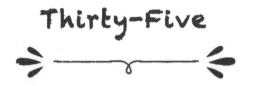

Susan hurried to throw away Ted's empty beer bottles before Allison arrived. *I couldn't have misheard her. I'm pretty damn sure she said she loved me.* She put on a pot of coffee and rushed to straighten up the living room. Positioning a throw pillow against the sofa's arm, she stopped as she found something small and white in the crevice between the cushions. *Are you fucking kidding me? When Ted gets back, I'm going to have a conversation about Sam. She can't be leaving her syringes in our house. Ugh. As if I didn't have enough to deal with that Adia bitch, now I have to deal with this. God fucking damn it.* She breathed and closed her eyes. *No, Susan, just put it away for now. Allie's coming over.* She opened her eyes as the doorbell rang. Hiding the syringe behind the DVDs, she ran to the door.

Allison was still wearing the outfit from earlier, but her hair was let down in soft waves on her shoulder. Rain was just beginning to fall, casting a sparkling glow upon the concrete and tree leaves as the sky darkened. "Would you like some coffee, Allie?"

"Yes, please." Allison began to step inside but withdrew her foot. "Let's have coffee out here."

"Okay." Susan made her way to the kitchen and poured two cups. She watched the steam rise and intermingle. She watched it fade in the air. *Okay, I can do this. I need to tell her. I need to kiss her. If I don't, we'll fade. I will fade.*

Susan opened the door to Allison leaning against the wooden pillar, watching the rain. She set the cups on the porch table as she watched Allison's hair move with the wind. The porch creaked as Susan approached her and ran her hand across her back. Allison turned her head, allowing her hair to move with the wind's will. Susan came closer. *'I love you.' That's what she said.* Looking into her eyes, she trembled and drew Allison closer. Their eyes closed as they melted into each other, lips meeting each other with soft hunger amid the scent of coffee and earth. Susan ran her fingers through her hair and Allison pulled her closer.

A car screeched its tires as it took off down the street, interrupting their embrace. Allison giggled and fell into Susan's embrace. *I have to tell her.* She trembled as she whispered, "I love you" into her ear. Allison smiled and ran her hand under the back of Susan's shirt. Susan drew her back into a kiss.

Allison's phone rang.

She ignored it.

It rang again.

And again.

"What the eff?" Allison looked down at the three missed calls.

It rang again.

"Answer it." Susan said.

"But I don't recognize the number."

"Why do they keep calling? Maybe it's an emergency."

"Okay." She put the phone to her cheek. "Hello?" Silence. "Hello?"

"I know where you are," said the voice on the other end.

Susan saw Allison freeze. The voice continued. "Yeah, it's me. I just saw you kissing that whore. I'm coming back."

Click.

Sure enough, the car came back around and parked in the yard. Adia got out, slammed the door and made her way to the couple. She swung at Susan. Susan grabbed her and pinned her to the porch floor. "Really, Adia, you think you can take me?"

"Why are you here, Adia?" Allison stood against the railing.

"You belong to me. I'm taking you back to

my place."

"No you're not."

"I've got a knife."

Susan strengthened her hold. "We've got a cell phone and we're calling the cops."

"They can't stop me from getting you. I will bring Allison back to me, even if I have to kill her."

"You're fucking insane."

Allison dialed 911.

Susan struggled with her grip as Adia tried to escape. She spat in Susan's face. "Fucking bitch. You don't know what it's like being me." She bared her teeth. "I'll fucking kill you if I have to. No one takes my women away. No one."

Susan just stared and held her there for a good fifteen minutes. Allison watched as the neighbors started to gather across the street. She glanced at her phone. *Come on, police. Get here.* She winced.

Soon flashing lights filled the neighborhood. *Perks of living in a somewhat shady neighborhood; the cops are super quick to respond.* Susan let go of Adia as soon as the cops got out of their car. Adia sprinted down the street, but the cops grabbed her.

"I'm going to kill her! You hear me?" she kept screaming as the officer handcuffed her and read her her rights.

"You'd think she'd stop saying that around the cops," Susan muttered to Allison.

"Yeah. You'd think." They both watched the police car pull away.

Thirty-Six

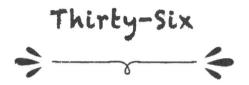

Allison sat on Susan's couch after the police collected their statements and left. *My life is so messed up.* Susan handed her a cup of hot cocoa. She blew on it and sipped. After savoring the sweet chocolate, she set the cup on the coffee table. *I feel lighter.* Susan sat next to her and set her cup next to Allison's. *She's so strong.* She cuddled up next to her and hugged her arm. "You have big muscles." She smiled.

"I work out." Susan flashed a grin her way.

Allison ran her finger along her inner thigh and watched as the other woman shifted in response. "You know what, Susan?"

"W…What?"

"I've been to your house many times, but I've never seen your bedroom." She moved her finger upwards.

"It's nothing special, but now that you mention it, it would be rude to *not* show you." Susan got up and pulled Allison by her arm. Allison fell toward her and landed against her chest. Susan began kissing her neck. "Come on." She led the other woman up the stairs and into her bedroom.

It's so messily charming. Allison closed the door and sat on the bed.

"It's not much, but I like it." Susan lit some candles and sandalwood filled the air. She sat on the bed.

"I like it," Allison whispered as she kissed Susan. Susan pulled her on top of her and took off Allison's t-shirt, revealing a black lace bra.

"Lace?" Susan asked as Allison sat on top of her.

"Of course, I love girly things." She giggled as she took her bra off.

Susan drew her close and kissed her hard. She pushed her down so that she was now on top. Susan kissed her way downward. Allison's nipples hardened as she kissed them. She gave a slight moan as Susan teased and nibbled her hip. She made her way back to her mouth and kissed her again as she slid her hand down her pants, but outside her underwear. "Lace again." Susan whispered into her ear.

Allison was overcome with longing. She ran her hands under Susan's shirt and caressed her back. Susan sat up and removed her shirt and sports bra. She returned to kissing her. The skin-on-skin contact was electrifying. They rolled over and Allison undid Susan's pants. She kissed her inner thigh, sending shivers up her spine. Running her finger along her plain, black panties, she could feel how much she wanted her. She couldn't control herself and removed them. Allison could feel the heat radiating upon her face. Her tongue explored every inch of Susan. She could feel her moans as she gyrated on her back. She brought her to the edge and stopped. Smiling to herself, Allison returned to kissing her inner thigh. Susan moaned in protest. Allison returned to her and she felt her stiffen inside her mouth. There was a loud gasp, but Allison kept going, causing her to stiffen again.

Allison traveled upward, kissing all the way to her neck. She smiled as she cuddled Susan.

"Wow, Allie. That was…" Susan breathed.

"Amazing?" giggled Allison.

"Yeah." Susan got on top of her. "Now let me return the favor."

Thirty-Seven

Sam sat in her bed, watching the cars go by from her window. Five stories below, they moved at a somewhat steady pace to the tune of traffic lights and rain. Rain. *I don't like rain.* She closed the blinds and went into the bathroom. She fussed with her hair for a bit before returning to her window. *I could just end it all now. He'd be happy I did.* "No," she said outloud to herself. "If I do that, he wins." She went to the kitchen and made some instant coffee. She could see his face. Blonde thinning hair. Glasses. She shook her head and grabbed her purse from the counter. Fishing for her supplies, she stopped. *Fuck! I forgot it at Ted's. Ugh.* She went to lie in bed. If she couldn't get her fix, she couldn't escape. She scrolled through her phone and texted her dealer. He said it'd be about two hours before he could deliver. She closed her eyes to take a quick nap.

She was back on her family's farm. It was a cold fall night and the stars shone against the dark trees lining their property. Sam felt the leaves crunch underneath her Power Ranger shoes. They lit up with each step and she smiled. She loved her shoes! Her father led her as she giggled. "Where are we going, Daddy?"

"Oh, just to those trees."

"Why?"

"I want to show you a family of bunny rabbits."

Sam laughed. "I love bunnies!"

"They're my favorite, too." Her father smiled, his shaggy blonde hair falling in his face.

They came to a clearing covered in leaves. She put her hands into her jacket. It was pink. Pink was her favorite color. "Where are the bunnies?"

Her father took something out of his pocket. "Here, you need to eat this before we see them or else they'll run away." He handed her some small tablets and a coke.

She washed them down and sat on a nearby log. Her vision blurred and she fell asleep.

The next day when she went to the bathroom, there was some blood on her underwear. I must have scratched myself wiping. *She shrugged and grabbed her favorite stuffed animal.*

Thirty-Eight

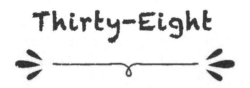

Ted was discharged from the hospital after a week. He woke the following morning at dawn in his own bed. He breathed in the fresh air from the open window. There was a faint scent of grass and chirping of birds. He rolled onto his side as he pushed aside his blankets. There was a heaviness about him, a silence in the room. Surveying the bedroom landscape, he rolled to his other side and scratched his stomach. He stared at the white bag of prescription drugs on his end table. *God damn it. Now I'm going to be a zombie. I'm not sick. I'm not ill. I don't need to take them.* He looked at his palms. *I can't believe I failed.* He looked at his door. *I need coffee.* He pulled on a shirt and a pair of jeans before heading downstairs and out the front door. *No need for breakfast; I'm not hungry.* He looked back at the house. It was a dark mountain against the rising sun. He noticed the curtains were shut in Susan's room. *I hope she has a good day. It's been rough for her. I can't imagine what it'd be like to have a failure as a friend.* He turned toward his car. *I'm going to walk today.*

He listened to the pounding of his sneakers against the concrete. Syncing them up to his heartbeat, he fell into the music of the morning. The grass and trees were still fuzzy with the grayness of the night. He kicked a rock. *I can't believe I failed.* He felt his head lower as he neared the intersection. He looked at his watch. 6:00 am. *The bus should be coming any time now.* Sure enough, the bus approached. Without thinking twice, he stepped into the street. The bus did not have enough time to stop. His glasses landed in the nearby bush.

Susan's phone rang in her pocket. She ignored it during the mid-morning rush. It rang again and she decided she should take the call. "Chris, I need to take five."

Chris nodded and took the next order as Susan stepped into the back room. She put her phone to her ear. "Hello?"

"Is this Susan?" said a male voice.

"Yes. Who is this?"

"This is Sergeant Bill Hanson from the Omaha Police Department." He paused. "I have news about your friend Ted Spencer."

"What happened? Is he okay?"

"We found his body in the bushes on 10th street. He was pronounced dead at the scene. We don't know all the details yet, but it looks like he was hit by a bus. We'll keep you informed."

"Thank you." She said in a monotone, and the officer ended the call. She stared at the screen and sat down on a box of coffee grounds. She put her hand to her forehead and convulsed into sobs. *This can't be happening. This can't be real. This can't be real. He can't be dead.*

Chris opened the door. "Sorry to interrupt, but I need some more Sumatra blend. Shit's selling like...shit." He stopped as he saw her crouched in the corner. "Are you ok?" He ran over and put his arm around her.

"T...Ted's...Ted's dead." She sobbed into his shoulder.

"What? I thought he was on anti-depressants now."

"No. He...He was hit...by a bus."

"Shit." He drew her closer. "Shit. Go home. I'll handle the shift today."

Susan ran out the back door, tears still streaming down her face. *This can't be real. This can't be real. This can't be real.* She ran to her car and fumbled with her keys. Unlocking it, she swung the door open, almost hitting the dumpster. She slid into the front seat and sunk into another convulsion.

Ten minutes passed before she was able to drive. Blaring *Bright Eyes*, she drove home. *Nobody should see me like this. I don't want anyone to see me like this.* She slammed her hand against the steering wheel as she was cut off. "God damn it, motherfucker!" she screamed as she swerved and righted herself. She sobbed. *I've been so caught up in my love life that I didn't pay more attention. I should have known he'd try again. I should have known. He's always been persistent. I'm so fucking selfish. I should have been more adamant about Sam. God. Fucking. Damn it.*

'I've found a liquid cure for my landlocked blues,' she heard Ted sing in her mind while sitting in the passenger seat. The memory disappeared as she switched the song to heavy metal. *I can't listen to his favorite music. I can't listen to mine. This is not real. This is not real.*

She pulled into her driveway. There was a silver Lexus parked in the front. Ted's brother was sitting on the porch, smoking a cigarette. *Ugh, I don't want to deal with his bullshit today.*

"Hey, Susan what's up?" He hopped down the steps and hugged her.

"You know what the fuck's up, Charlie." Susan squirmed out of his arms.

Charlie laughed. "I just wanted to see you."

Susan stormed toward the porch, stopped, and turned around. "Why the fuck are you here?"

221

"To comfort you." He followed her.

"Bullshit."

He put his hands over his heart and outstretched them. "Ah! You misunderstand!"

Susan dangled her keys in her hand. "Why are you here? You've never cared enough to even speak to me before. Why are you suddenly at my doorstep?"

Charlie put his hands into his jeans and leaned against the porch railing. His grin faded. "I feel bad."

"Why?" Susan watched his grin fade into nothing.

"I gave him so much fucking shit." He took out his lighter and turned it over in his hand. Charlie shook his head and met her eyes. "I've lost both my siblings. I'm alone."

Susan watched him turn into a child as tears welled up in his eyes. She gave him a hug as he lost it.

Thirty-Nine

"Hey, Chris!" Allison beamed as she strode into Cool Beans. Her bag rustled at her side with every step she took as she crossed the seating area. She looked around. "Where's Susan?"

Chris wiped a mug and set it down. The rush had tapered off and now only a few students were typing away at their laptops in the corner. "She went home," he said to the mug.

Something's wrong. "What happened?"

Chris put his hands on the counter. "Ted died."

Allison stepped closer and tilted her head. "What?"

"Ted died." He looked down and wiped away an imaginary spill. "The police called her about an hour ago."

Allison clutched her bag as her eyes widened. "Is she okay?"

"I don't know." His eyes glistened. "She took off in a hurry."

Allison took a step backward. *I need to be with her.*

Chris stopped fussing with the towel. "Go,

Allie, you need to be with her."

Her ballet flats clacked as she ran out of the shop. The students turned their heads and returned to their studies as the glass door closed. *Shit. Of course something bad would happen after things had been so good.* She put on some *Bright Eyes* and sped toward Susan's house. "We are nowhere and it's now," she sang as she saw Ted walking down the street. Allison blinked and he was gone. Her heart sunk. *I must be in shock.*

She pulled up and shuddered at the tracks left by Adia's car. Parking behind Susan's car, she got out and steeled herself. *I never know what to say to grieving people.* She saw Susan sitting on the porch with Ted's brother. She could smell the faint scent of coffee beans from their full cups. *Susan looks like a mess and so does Charlie.* Allison ran up the steps and hugged Susan.

"I heard what happened," she said into Susan's hair. "I'm…I'm so sorry."

Susan drew her closer.

Allison let go and turned to hug Charlie. "I'm sorry for your loss, Charlie. I know we don't know each other well, but I can't imagine how it must be to lose another sibling so soon after the other."

"It…it was over a decade ago." Charlie looked through his coffee. "It's probably his own fault. But I can't shake this feeling of guilt. I've never much liked him, but he *was* my brother, after all."

Allison placed one hand on Susan's shoulder. "That's still too soon." She rubbed her shoulder. *Life's too short.*

The cows mooed as Ted took out his thermos and two paper cups. Pouring two cups of instant latte, he handed one to his friend and chugged his own. He looked down at his cup and tossed it in the backseat of his car. He looked at the cows and climbed the ancient, wooden fence. Sitting down on the cracked post, he watched Susan sip her drink. "Life is like coffee. It swirls and bubbles, encapsulating our collective experiences in a flavorful sip and spilling warmth into our soul, each person adding another dimension of intricacy to the brew. To get the most flavor, we must take our coffee black. Therefore, in order to experience life's true nature, it's true uninhibited nature, we must avoid tainting it with unnecessary additions. However, we must drink it before it gets cold and stale. We must live our youth pure and unadulterated, like that of black coffee. Like that of acoustic music. We must live the life acoustic." Ted stood up on the fencepost as Su-

san leaned against his Cadillac, drinking a caramel latte.

"That's very profound, Ted." Susan cocked her head. Two birds cawed above. She emptied the paper cup and threw it in the car.

"Well, I'm feeling profoundly profound today, Suze." He jumped down, red flannel shirt hitting his back. He chuckled and hugged her. "We're graduates now!"

Susan laughed. "Not yet! Tomorrow's graduation."

"Well, we're practically graduates." He punched the air. "We're finally free of the papers and Greeks!"

Susan shook her head. "The Greeks never really bothered me, or the papers for that matter." She pointed to herself. "English major. Duh."

"I know, but we're supposed to be happy." He sat on the hood of his car.

Susan sat down next to him. "Yeah, we're supposed to feel happy." She leaned back on her hands. "I don't feel truly happy, though." She looked at her feet. "I feel more afraid than anything."

Ted leaned back and looked up at the clouds. "Me, too. I'm afraid of what's going to happen. What's going to happen to us, Susan? Will we still be friends a year from now? Will you find *love?" He sighed. "So many questions." He reached toward the sky. "Such uncertainty."*

Susan woke up with Allison beside her. She watched her slow breaths as she sat up and gathered her robe. She looked at the dark mass in her hands. *Well, I guess I don't really need this since Ted's gone.* Drawing it close to her, she cried for a moment. *Why do I think things like that? I should be sadder.* The robe fell to the floor and she left the bed and headed downstairs. The creaking stairs echoed in the silent house. *I hope I don't wake Allie.* She poured a glass of water and gulped it down. Looking out the kitchen window, she saw memories flash by her.

Susan gripped the counter and felt a hand grip her arm. "Ted, go to bed," she said out of habit, but it was Allison. Susan fell against her chest and allowed her to stroke her hair. "I'm sorry I woke you, Allie."

"You didn't. I had a bad dream." Allison kissed her head.

"I'm sorry." Susan hugged her.

"It's okay."

"What did you dream about?" Susan lifted her head.

"These two creepy birds and a Cadillac." Allison let her go and poured her own glass of water. "It was so weird. There were these two people I didn't know just chilling in the country and I was trapped in a cave with these super creepy birds threatening me."

Susan almost dropped the glass she was holding.

Forty

Sam was lying in bed when she heard the door knock. It was a single knock, loud and abrasive. She looked through the peephole and saw no one. Opening the door with a slight creak, she stepped barefoot onto the hallway's industrial carpet. No one was there. *Dammit Mike, get here.* She went back to her living room and turned on her TV.

She reclined in the blue armchair and watched the mindless reality show through half-glazed eyes. Sam yawned and scrolled through her phone as the door knocked again. This time it was Mike.

"Wanna come in for a drink?" she offered.

"Naw, I got another client waiting, but thanks for the offer." He handed her a small bag.

She got out her pocketbook, but he waved it away. "What?"

"It's free tonight."

"Why?"

"I'm feeling generous."

She narrowed her eyes. "If anything fucked up happens, I'm blaming you."

"Ha ha. Okay." He smiled as he left.

Sam eyed the bag with caution. She shook it against the light and frowned. With a dull thud, she threw it in the trash. *I don't have time for tainted shit.* She took her phone from her pocket and dialed Ted. No answer. She checked the time. *Oh well, might as well go grab a few beers with the band. It's still early, so I can still get smashed.* She dialed her drummer and set her plans in motion.

Sam woke up with the drummer in the bed. *Oh man, what did I do last night?* She groaned as she grabbed a wadded up outfit from the floor. She texted Ted and ate a small bowl of cereal before she vomited in the bathroom. It was almost noon.

An hour passed and she still hadn't received a "good morning" text from her boyfriend. *Ugh, what if he found out I took another man home.* She threw up at the thought. Sam kicked her companion out and poured some coffee. An unknown number called her phone. She ignored it. *I should go over to Ted's, but he's probably at work.* She added some sugar to her coffee. *I feel so horrible. I don't even know if I had sex with*

230

Jake last night. God damn it.

Another hour passed. Still no text. *Damn it. Where is he? This is bullshit. I need to talk to him.* She brushed her hair, left her apartment, and headed to Ted's. On her way, she passed what looked like a crime scene. Her stomach lurched as she saw blood and she pulled over and vomited on the concrete. Sam wiped her mouth and continued on her way. *Why is his car there? He should be at work. Maybe I lucked out.* She parked across the street and met the others on the porch.

"Why so glum? It looks like someone died." She grinned as she took off her sunglasses.

Allison was playing with Susan's hair as she spoke. "Ted died."

"No he didn't. You're fucking with me." Sam turned to the other man. "Why are you here?"

He looked at his cup and at her. "Because Ted died."

Susan nodded.

"Oh shit." Sam braced herself against the house. "Oh shit. Oh shit. Oh shit."

Forty-One

Allison sat on the red padded chair. Her hands grazed the rough fabric as she crossed her legs. *Wakes are weird. Everyone comes to look at a dead body.* She stared at the bearded, lifeless face amid the cream-colored lining and polished wood. Turning to her side, she looked at Susan's face. *She's not crying.* She sighed inward. *I wish I had her composure.* She looked back at the casket and then to the floor. *Well, I guess I can maybe learn to be composed under stress.* A hymn was playing in the background of flowers and mourners. *So many people. Most of them look middle-aged or older. Ted's family must have a lot of friends. I'm not really surprised; they're pretty big around here.* Allison took in the surroundings. *I hope when I die, I can have this many people show up.* She felt a pressure on her hand. Susan pressed harder and let go.

"Allie, I think we can leave now." Susan gave a forced half-smile. "It's been an hour and I'm kinda hungry." She stood up and grabbed her bag, slipping it over the shoulder of her black pantsuit.

She looks so good tonight. Allison couldn't help checking her out. *Ugh, I shouldn't be doing this here.* She averted her eyes as she, too, got up and ready to go. She waited until they left the parlor to speak. "Where do you want to go for dinner? I'll pay."

"You don't have to do that." Susan slowed her pace to match Allison's. "Let's try out that new pizza place. It's been so long, okay maybe a month or so, since I've had a good slice that didn't taste like cardboard."

Allison gave a slight giggle as she took Susan's hand and crossed the street to her car. "You look really nice tonight. Suits suit you."

Susan looked at the car, "I'm glad you think so. I feel like a monkey right now."

"A sexy monkey." *I shouldn't be talking like this so soon after a wake. I must be getting my period soon. I can't stop thinking about sex.* Allison got into the car. *She probably doesn't want to have any tonight anyway.* Allison watched Susan's wrists as they drove the mile or so to the restaurant. *I wonder if she has toys. Her wrists are really toned.* Allison turned her attention to the road ahead. *No, she's a barista. Her wrists get a workout at work. I should really stop thinking about sex right now. Think about pizza. Pizza is delicious. Pizza is life.*

The car came to a stop a few feet from the

door. "Awesome spot, Susan!"

"I do what I can."

They opened the door to a wide dining area. The booths and tables were set with traditional red-and-white-checkered table clothes. The host led them to a booth in the corner, far away from the noisy families by the door. *Good, this is more intimate.*

"Hi, I'm Jose and I'll be your server tonight. Can I start you off with something to drink?" He took out two menus from his apron pouch.

Allison took the menus and handed one to Susan. "I'll have a Coke."

"I'll have a beer. What do you have on tap?"

Jose drew his hands toward his body. "We have Budweiser, Bud Light, Corona, and Heineken."

"I'll have Budweiser."

"Alright. I will be back shortly to take your order." He jotted down the drinks on his notepad and scampered toward the kitchen.

"Too bad they don't have PBR." Allison mused.

"Yeah, they get five cool points taken away." Susan scanned the menu. "What type of pizza do you want?"

Allison looked at hers. "The Hawaiian looks really good." She smiled. "I love pineapple."

Susan chuckled. "Then it's decided." She

closed her menu and set it aside.

The waiter returned with their drinks and took their order. "He seems friendly enough." Allison said as she sipped her Coke.

"Yeah." Susan took her palm and gave it a gentle rub. "I'm really glad you came to the wake with me. I couldn't have done it without you. Thank you."

Allison warmed. *She's so, so polite. I definitely upgraded.* She smiled and cradled her chin in her opposite hand. "You're welcome."

She was lost for a moment in Susan's eyes. *She's so amazing. I...I think she is good for me.*

She didn't notice the man approach the table. "Can I help you?" Susan asked as she withdrew her hand. The man had a slight but muscular build with a well-manicured goatee. His jeans looked brand new and his green t-shirt drew attention to his pectorals.

"Hi, my name is Tom and I think your friend is beautiful." He grinned a sleazy grin as he turned his head to Allison.

Eww... "I'm sorry." She glanced at Susan. "I'm taken."

The man leaned on the booth and ran his hand through her hair. "I'm pretty sure I'll treat you better than your boyfriend."

Allison backed away from him and his alcohol tinged breath. "Uh...No you couldn't."

"Aw come on." He sat down.

Susan stood up. "Sir, please leave her alone."

"Just sit down. You're screwin' up my game." He gestured for her to leave.

Susan took a few steps forward. "She's with me."

The guy looked her up and down. He laughed. "I know you're here with her, but her boyfriend isn't." He swayed a bit.

"No. She's my girlfriend." She tilted her head. "Now leave before I tell the manager."

Allison saw anger well up in her eyes.

Tom got out of the booth and stood up. "Make me." He swung at her.

Susan dodged and he fell head first into a table, sending silverware and condiments flying, getting everyone's attention.

"You fuckin' dyke." He struggled to get off the floor. His friends came over and guided him back to his seat. The head waitress came over and fixed the table.

"I'm so sorry that happened," she apologized. "We want every dining experience to be the best, so consider your next meal on us."

"Well at least something good came out of this." Allison relaxed a bit as she watched Tom and his friends leave. *I can't believe that actually happened. Oh wait, yes I can. This is the third time she's protected me. I really need to learn to protect myself.*

Susan sat down. "Yeah, I guess." She moved her glass out of the way as Jose set down the steaming pizza in the center of the table.

"That's the third time you've saved me." Allison took a bite and let the cheese fall down in strings on her plate.

"Well, I do what I can." Susan gave a weak smile as she folded her slice.

"You're awesome, you know that?" *I really want to thank her...appropriately.* She gave a half smile as she watched her eat. *Ugh...I'm so pathetic.* She gave a small laugh and sipped on her Coke. "Hey Susan, what do you want to do after this?"

"I don't know. Maybe go home and relax? This week's been stressful." Susan wiped her hands on her napkin.

"Yeah, it has been. Do you like bubble baths?" *Mmmmm...Susan amid candlelight and bubbles.* She fidgeted with the hanging table-cloth.

Susan picked up the check as the waiter set it down. Sliding her debit card into the plastic pocket, she looked up at her. "You know, it's been a long time since I've had one."

"I said I'd pay for dinner." Allison swirled her straw.

"You can make it up to me later." Susan slid

her hand under the table and ran her fingers over Allison's knees, causing goosebumps to run up her spine.

"C...can we make a stop on the way home?" Allison composed herself.

"Sure." Susan smiled at Jose as he picked up the check. "Where?"

"Oh, just Target. I want to get some candles and bath salts."

"You know I've never taken a bath with someone. Do you think there would be enough room?"

"Well...we don't need to take a bath together, although I'd really like it." Allison felt her face blush. "I just want you to be able to relax. Maybe I could give you a massage?" *Yes, a massage...with rose petals.* Allison had to will herself not to drool in public.

Susan reclined in the bath and let the water splash over her body, causing the candles' reflections to ripple in the steamy water. She felt the heat discover her shoulders and neck as she submerged her head. *Allie is a genius.* She brought her head out of the water and opened her eyes. Rose petals floated back and forth. *I wish*

this tub were big enough for two people. She imagined Allison beside her, brown hair floating amid hers. *Mmmm...* She took in the scent of patchouli. *I wonder what she's doing right now.* Susan took out her lavender body wash. She smoothed it over her body and rinsed off the suds.

She stepped out of the bath and took a plush towel from the rack above the sink. Drying herself, she blotted her hair and stepped out of the bathroom. She was greeted with cold air and goosebumps. *I should have worn the towel.* She crossed her arms as she walked down the hallway. Upon entering the bedroom, she was greeted by more candles and incense. The light was dim and there were rose petals on the bed. *Now I know why she bought the value pack.* She searched the room for Allison. *Where is she hiding?* Susan felt silk around her eyes.

"Don't worry. It's just me." Allison purred in her ear.

Susan felt a trail of kisses down her neck, causing more goosebumps. "You're cunning." Susan smiled.

"Shhh...Just follow me." Allison took her hand and led her to the bed. "Lie on your stomach."

Susan acquiesced. *Oh, yeah. I bet she's great at massages.* She arched her back as cold oil dripped onto her skin.

"Don't worry, it warms up." Allison whispered to her as she slid her hand up and down her spine.

Allison felt her breast brush against her own. *Mmm...She's naked, too.* She lost herself in ecstasy. Susan groaned as Allison removed the blindfold. "Where did you learn how to do that?" She turned over on her back.

Allison smirked and twirled her hair. "Did you forget that I'm an artist? Naturally, I'm good with my hands." She kissed her with such fervor that Susan clutched her comforter.

Susan woke up at dawn to Allison cradled against her breast. She stared up at the ceiling and played with her lover's hair. *Today is the day.* She sighed and Allison let out a slight groan as she cuddled up closer. Susan looked down at her. *She's so beautiful in the morning.* She took a strand of her hair between her fingers and let it fall down. Susan looked up at the ceiling again and closed her eyes. *I don't want to go to the church today. I just want to lie here with her forever. Can I just pretend that my friend's funeral isn't today? Can I just wish him back into exis-*

tence?

She felt Allison's hand take hold of hers. The softness of her palms sent warmth throughout her body. She opened her eyes to Allison's. Allison kissed her and let her lips linger.

"Good morning." Allison whispered.

Susan slid her hand across her bare back. "I wish it was." She took her other hand and lifted Allison's chin. "Can we just lay here forever and not go to the funeral?"

"Oh, baby…" Allison hugged her closer. "I wish I could make your pain go away." She ran her fingers across her stomach, causing Susan's back to arch.

"I think you can." Susan kissed her and pulled her on top of herself.

They made love as the sun rose and illuminated the room. Sweat glistened in the sunlight afterward as they cradled each other amongst the disheveled blankets.

Susan glanced at the clock. *Three hours. Three hours until I bury my best friend.* She pulled Allison closer and kissed her through her sweaty hair.

"Shall we shower?" Allison grinned.

Susan nodded and ran her hand through her hair. She watched Allison walk nude to the bathroom. "I'll join you in a minute, Allie." *I need to get through today. I need to do this. I need to be strong.* She let tears fall down her cheek. They intermingled with the sweat and dampened her pillow. She rolled out of bed and wiped her eyes. Feeling the steam of the shower from the bathroom down the hall, she placed her hand on the wall to steady herself. *I'm weak, though.* She made it to the bathroom and saw her girlfriend's silhouette through the shower curtain. *I need to appear strong. For her. For myself.* She slid the curtain open and felt the hot water on her shoulder.

After breakfast and dressing, the two women headed to St. Cecelia's Cathedral. The Spencer's didn't spare any expense for their eldest son's funeral. The altar was lined with bushels and bushels of red roses and lilies. The pews were almost full by the time they arrived. *I wonder if it's appropriate if I sit by the family. So many people.* Susan saw Chris sitting next to some of the guys from the party. *Those must be Ted's classmates. I should meet up with Chris later.* She spied Ted's mom chatting with Charlie towards the front of the massive room. Susan gave a gentle wave and Mrs. Spencer motioned for her to come closer. Allison fell back a few steps and

Susan turned and grabbed her hand. They walked hand in hand up the aisle.

Mrs. Spencer gave Susan a big hug. Tears smeared her makeup as she brushed against the younger woman. "I'm so…so sorry for your loss, Mrs. Spencer." Susan hugged her back.

"Susan, you meant so much to Teddy. He talked about you constantly. We all thought he'd marry you." She withdrew her arms. "Please, sit next to us." Her eyes discovered Allison. "You too, dear." She pulled Allison into the pew. "Charlie, go help the others." Mrs. Spencer waved her son away. The two women sat down on the cold, padded wood. The matron wiped her tears as she went to greet some relatives.

Susan turned to Allison and laid her hand on her knee. "Mrs. Spencer is really nice. I don't know how she's dealing with the loss of another child."

"I know. It's so sad." Allison turned toward her.

"Yeah. It was pretty rough on Ted." She looked at the altar. There was a picture of all three children near the center. "I don't think he ever got over it." She looked back at Allison. "The media coverage sure didn't help."

"Media?" Allison arched her eyebrow.

"Yeah, it was a pretty big deal. His sister was an all-star basketball player who was shot by her ex-boyfriend." Susan watched Mrs. Spencer hug Ted's father. "It was all over the local stations for months."

Allison followed her gaze. "Now that you mention it…" Organ music cut her off and the Spencer's sat back down. "I've never been to a Catholic funeral."

"They're interesting and long." Susan forced a smile. She looked around. "I don't see Sam, Allie. I wonder where she is? Do you think she is shooting up right now?"

"I wouldn't be surprised." Allison muttered.

The back doors opened and the pallbearers carried the casket up the aisle as a hymn poured out from the organ. The white pall was embroidered with gold crosses and stood out against the overwhelming black wardrobe of the congregation as they rose to their feet. Susan's heart sank and she grasped Allison's hand. *This is too much. This. Is. Too. Much.* She buried her head in Allison's shoulder and wept. She lifted her head and watched the casket creep past and gripped Allison's hand tighter. Soon, the Archbishop blessed it with incense and began the Mass.

The next hour was full of somber liturgy and hymns. Susan could not keep her eyes off of the casket. *Ted's in there. His body is probably cold. I wonder if he's happy now. I wonder if he can see us. I wonder if he's free. I wonder if Livi is with him.* She held Allison's hand, not paying any attention to the side-glances from the crowd.

Be Not Afraid started as the Archbishop ended the Mass and began the recession. One by one, the rows followed the pallbearers out of the cathedral.

Susan stood with the family as Ted was carried to the open back of a shiny black hearse. Charlie lost his grip, causing them to almost drop the casket on the stairs.

Oh, God. Susan stepped out of the crowd and came to Charlie's aide. "I'll help."

Charlie nodded and waved the youngest pallbearer, Ted's youngest cousin, away. Susan took the handle and they resumed the recession. The organ music resounded as they headed, step by step, to the hearse.

Susan looked down at Ted's casket. More tears came. She wiped them away with her free hand. *I hope you liked the funeral. It was nice.* She gave a fleeting smile through her tears. They loaded him into the back of the hearse, and Susan motioned for the cousin to take back his post.

Allison met her at the bottom of the stairs and took her arm. They stood there for a moment as they watched the men close the hearse. "Let's find our car." She gave a tug.

"O...okay."

Forty-Two

Sam sat in her chair. *I should go to the funeral.* She looked at the clock and shook her head. *No, I can't meet his family. Not like this.* She wept into her hands. *I can't meet his fucking family at his fucking funeral.* Her stash sat on the end table. She threw it across the room. "This is all my fucking fault!" she screamed through sobs. "Damn it! Why do I always fuck up my life?"

She stood up and rushed to get dressed. *I have to fucking go.* She stopped and inhaled, tasting salt. *I have to. I have to do this.* She ran out the door, not caring about her messy hair. Speeding, she arrived at the cathedral as the procession ended. Creeping along the back, she found an empty seat and genuflected. *I haven't been in a church since...since I was a kid. But here I am remembering the traditions.* She smiled to herself.

She spotted Susan and Allison up front. *Susan looks like hot mess. I guess Ted was really like a brother to her. Funny how someone as strong as her could break down like that.* Sam shifted her feet. She felt another rush of sadness overtake her. *I can't be here. I don't belong here.* She got up and left without a sound. *No one probably noticed that I was there. But I paid my dues.* She drove down the street to the convenience store and bought a handle of Jack Daniels. *I should go to the cemetery and pour one out for him. But he's not there yet. Damn. I will go there tonight.*

She got in her car and started the engine. *No, I have to see Susan. I must make amends. I must be strong.* She turned the bottle over in her hands. *I can't do this anymore.* She turned off her car and opened the door. Opening the bottle, she poured the contents onto the asphalt.

She shook out the last drops and headed back to the funeral.

Forty-Three

Allison drove Susan to the cemetery. The funeral procession was long and took almost an hour to arrive at the cemetery. *Wow, this family really does go all out.* She glanced at her girlfriend in the passenger seat and grabbed her hand. "I love you, Susan." She squeezed it.

"I don't think I can do the burial." Susan watched the buildings go by.

"You don't have to, baby. I can leave the procession and head home."

"No." Susan faced Allison. "I want to see him laid to rest. I just…I just don't think I can handle the burial ceremony."

"Oh…Okay. Well," she gave her hand another squeeze, "we can watch it from a distance." *She's trying so hard to be strong. I don't think she realizes just how strong she is.* "Take your phone out, Susan, and put on some *Bright Eyes.* Ted would love that."

Susan hooked her phone up to the stereo and acoustic music soon took over the car. She laid her head back and closed her eyes. "I really do love you, Allie."

Allison smiled and turned up the volume.

A crowd of about forty assembled around the grave. The black casket reflected the distorted faces as it was prepared to be lowered. As the people approached, more faces stretched and bled together into one mosaic under the blue sky. The grass added a splash of emerald to the blacks and grays. The surrounding limestone and gran-ite gravestones were welcoming the addition of Ted, another life martyr.

Susan trudged through the short grass to the Spencer plot. It was mowed just for the occasion. Her flats felt the soft brush as she continued past wrought iron gates and fragrant pines. Her heart pounded with each step. She saw the crowd gathered in the distance. The priest wasn't there yet. *I've arrived just in time. Just in time to bury my best friend.* She hung her head as she ran her fingers along a rough antique stone.

Allison followed a few steps behind her. Su-san leaned against the tall stone as the other woman caught up to her. Allison's dress fluttered as she approached. Susan raised her head and met her reflection in sunglassed eyes. *I look hor-rible. I knew I shouldn't have worn mascara.*

Allison took off her sunglasses and walked up to Susan. The blonde stood against the pines and the sky like a sorrowful guardian angel. Allison inched closer and took her hand. It was warm. She looked up into the mascara-tainted tears and brought her other hand around Susan's head. The wind rustled the pines as lips met with a fusion of sadness and passion.

Susan smelled the faint fragrance of patchouli as Allison's hair mingled with her own.

"I love you." Allison said as Susan held her.

"I love you too." Susan caressed her hair as she saw a ghostly hipster in the woods. She started and rubbed her eyes.

"What's wrong?" Allison looked up.

"Nothing, just saw a rabbit." She drew her back to her breast. The sweet smell of the pines and the breeze enveloped them as they stood there until the service ended and the people dispersed.

"Should we go to the reception?" Allison asked as she let go of Susan.

"No. Those people didn't know the real Ted. Let's get Chris and a six pack of PBR." She straightened Allison's dress. "Then let's go to my house and pour one out for him. He'd like that." The grass and pine needles sank with their footsteps as they made their way to Susan's car.

They drove down the gravel road and through the cemetery gate as they blared Ted's favorite songs.

Forty-Four

Allison stood in the checkout line at Target. She clutched the red spray paint in her right hand. *I need to do something simple, something positive. Suicide sucks. Death sucks.* She put the can on the counter and swiped her debit card. The doors swished as she left the store. A cool breeze provided some respite from the humidity, but caused her floral dress to whip against her legs. A sigh of irritation escaped her lips.

A car slowed down beside her and rolled down its window. "Hey, baby. Where you going?"

Allison stopped, almost dropping the spray can. *That voice. No. She was arrested.* She hurried to her car. The car followed. She dropped her keys as she opened her door and she heard the other car's engine stop, trapping her in the parking space. *Are you kidding me?*

"Just come here. I want to talk." Adia said through the window.

"Aren't you supposed to be in jail?" Allison opened the car door.

"A friend posted bail." Adia turned on her

hazards and got out. She stood at the front of her car.

"You have friends?" Allison shut her door and locked it. *Please just leave.*

Adia came closer. "Oh, believe me, I'm still going to trial. I'm sorry I said those things to you. I was acting out of character. I love you and I need you, Allison."

"No you don't." Allison started to roll up her window, but Adia stuck her hands between the door and the window. *She's insane.*

"Yeah, I do. I could love you a whole lot better than that bitch. You know this."

"Go away."

"No." Adia tried to open the door. "You need to come with me."

"Get the HELL away from me!" Allison shouted, causing passersby to stop and stare.

Adia glanced around. "Nothing to see here." She started to back away and got in her car. "Oh Allison, I saw that spray can. I know your secret."

The car sped out of the parking lot and Allison shook as she grabbed her cell phone and dialed Susan. "Hey, I'm coming over."

She backed out of the parking space and took the back roads to Susan's. *Hopefully, she isn't crazy enough to follow me. Who am I kidding? She is, but it's better to be with someone who can kick butt than alone in my apartment.* She looked over her shoulder and made sure no one followed her up to the door.

When Susan answered, she ran inside. "Adia's out. Someone posted her bail."

"What?" Susan furrowed her brow.

"I ran into Adia just now at Target."

Susan rolled her eyes. "Just another thing we have to worry about." She came over and hugged Allison. "Did she follow you here?"

"Not to my knowledge. You better lock the doors anyway." Allison sat down and crossed her legs.

"Done and done." Susan locked the front door and left to secure the back door.

Allison played with her dress. *Adia knows what I'm doing. What if she tells the cops? Ugh. I need a contingency plan.*

"Alright, Allie." Susan came back into the room. "I've secured all the windows. I'm so glad that we, I mean, I have a security system."

I should tell her. Susan sat down beside her. *No, I need to tell her. I don't want secrets in this relationship.* "Hey, Susan." She sat up and turned toward her. "I need to tell you something."

Susan shifted on the couch cushion. "What's up?"

Allison looked at her lap and fiddled with her

hands. "So...uh...you know that ninja artist that's been all over the news?"

"Yeah. She's pretty cool. I like her work." Susan relaxed a little.

"Well...uh...I'm that ninja artist."

"Get out! No way! Really?" Susan's eyes lit. "That's awesome!" She stopped. "You're not fucking with me, are you?"

Allison met her eyes. "No, I'm not."

Susan's eyes widen and she kissed Allison. *Well, that was a better reaction than expected.*

"You see, I didn't want any secrets in this relationship. Lord knows the one I had with Adia was unhealthy enough for everyone in this city." Allison leaned against Susan. "Also, there's a chance that she might tell the police and have them arrest me."

Susan placed her arm over her. "I think you should lay low for a while. Let the fervor die down and then strike again...with a vengeance." Susan forced a laugh.

She's trying so hard to be happy right now. I can't imagine how it must be to bury a friend. Allison snuggled closer. "You know he's still with us."

"Yeah. I can feel him here." Susan stared through the doorway. "To be cliché, I think he always will be. You don't get to know someone that well to only have them forgotten in a few months." She frowned. "I feel guilty. I should have taken better care of him."

"You guys were super close." Allison rubbed Susan's arm. "But please don't blame yourself. At least try not to. He just fought a battle too hard for him."

Susan started to cry. "He was like a brother to me." She paused. "You know, I think he knew I was gay before me." Susan stopped crying. She laughed and placed her hand to her forehead. Her laughter turned to sobs again as Allison hugged her arm. They sat there until Susan fell asleep.

Allison got up and turned out the kitchen lights. She opened the door to Ted's room and turned on the lights. *It's so surreal. Just the other day, someone lived here.* Her eyes traveled from the bed to the discarded whiskey bottles to the pictures on the end table. She sat on the bed and ran her fingers along the fabric. The tree branch rustled against the window, causing a loud scraping noise. Allison winced. Some wind must have leaked into the room, because the closet door closed. She reclined on the bed. "I know you're here," she whispered to the ceiling. "You don't have to worry, I'll take care of her."

She leaned over and spied a stack of books on the floor. Picking one up, she read the title *The Over-Soul and other Essays*. Allison flipped open the cover and a piece of paper fell out. She unfolded it, revealing a selfie of Ted and Susan on the hood of Ted's Cadillac. She turned it over and read.

We are all connected.
We are never apart.
Family forever.

Forty-Five

Adia stood in her kitchen doorway, crying. *Why can't I have her back? It's not fair. It's not fucking fair.* She slammed her fist through the drywall. Yellow paint chips and plaster fell to the ground as she pulled her bleeding hand from the wall. She watched the blood drip onto the shag carpet, its redness melting into the ash brown. *I have an idea.* She pulled some paper towels off the spool and blotted her hand. Laughing to herself, she snapped a picture of her injury and sent it to Allison. *I'm going to make it seem like I'm going to kill myself. She won't be able to live with the guilt of her true love's death and she'll ditch that bitch and come running back to me.* She laughed louder and fixed a cup of coffee.

No one gets away from me. No one. I've always gotten what I've wanted and I will continue to do so. No one can stop me—no one. She thought back to her dad and smiled. She always got a new car every year or so courtesy of him. She always had money. Always had everything. *I get whatever the fuck I want.*

Adia took her phone out and checked her messages. Nothing. *What the fuck? Why hasn't she responded? Any decent person would. Jesus fucking Christ. What the hell is wrong with people nowadays? They don't care about suicide at all. Motherfuckers.* She threw her phone at the wall. It bounced off and left a dent. She walked over and picked up the pieces. *I need to fucking make her pay.* She paced her living room and shook her hands. *I need to make her suffer.* She stopped in the middle of the room and looked through the window to the building across the street. *I need to make her suffer for what she's done to me.* Adia took a beer out of her mini fridge and chugged it. *I could tell the cops that she's the artist terrorizing the town, but she's probably expecting that and has covered her tracks. Besides, I don't actually have any proof.* She threw the empty beer bottle in the trash with a loud shatter. *Well, I could hurt Susan. She's already lost one friend. That could break her. No, it needs to be more substantial. Ted wasn't really anything to her anyway, just Susan's friend or whatever.* Adia got up and went back to the kitchen. *I know what to do.* She opened the drawer and took out a large steak knife. *I'll cut her.* She studied the knife in her hand. Rubbing her thumb over the wooden handle, she imagined what it'd be like to slice Susan's face. *If I can't overpower her, I'll disfigure her so badly that Allison won't be attracted to her anymore.* She set the knife on the counter and went into her bedroom. *I need to plan this out.* Opening her closet door, she took out her most revealing dress and felt its red silk. It was a backless mini dress that her previous ex had bought her. She grinned. *This is dress that I wore when I first met Allison.* She laid it down on the bed. *Now, I can't do this tonight. It'd be too obvious after what happened at Target tonight. Will wait a few days.* She crawled underneath her comforter and traced the hearts. *After all, I have to surprise her.*

Forty-Six

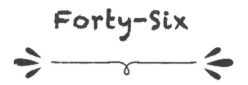

Susan woke to the faint smell of coffee. She sat up on the couch and stretched. *Who's in the kitchen?* She got up, folded the fleece blanket, and met Allison.

"Good morning, baby!" Allison set a plate full of scrambled eggs and hot sauce on the table and pulled out a chair. "How did you sleep?" She broke a few more eggs into the skillet and added some cheddar cheese.

Susan rubbed her eyes. "I…slept…ok." She pulled out an aged wooden chair and sat down at the table. Her girlfriend handed her a cup of coffee. "How did you?"

"I slept like a rock." She made herself a plate and turned off the burner. "I fell asleep pretty quickly." She forked her eggs. "Actually, I don't think I've slept that well in a long, long time."

"Well, my bed *is* pretty comfy." Susan smiled. *It feels pretty nice to have a woman wake up in my bed. Too bad I slept on the couch. Well, there's always tonight.* She poured more hot sauce on her eggs.

"Well." Allison poured herself some coffee.

"Actually, I slept in Ted's room."

What? Susan put down her fork with a clang. *That's kinda creepy. I haven't been in there since...since that day.*

"I went into his room to make sure the window was closed—you know, what with the Adia situation—and I found a book." She sat down opposite Susan and cocked her head. "I think it was *The Over-Soul* by Ralph Waldo Emerson." Allison took a bite of food. "It was pretty dry and I guess I fell asleep while reading." Her eyes widen. "Oh, I found something else!" She got up and ran upstairs to Ted's room. Thirty seconds later she was back at the table.

What's this? Susan took a folded piece of paper from her hand. Unfolding it, she studied the two people in the photo. "Oh hey, this is from the day before graduation. We went out for a drive in the Missouri countryside." Susan paused. "We had a special spot that we'd often go to with our other friends. We called it 'The Circle.' It was this weird cave-like place where witches did rituals." She smiled. "At least that was the local legend. It was true that Wiccans often gathered there, but it was really just a normal hangout in the middle of the country. Then again," she shrugged, "those memories *were* magical. Anyway, we thought we'd see it one more time before we left. These pesky crows kept bothering us, though."

"Turn it over, Susan." Allison sat down again.

Susan read the writing on the back. *Oh my God.* She stared at it for a moment and set it down beside her cup. *I must not cry. I've done too much crying.* "We...we really were...are... family." She let out a loud laugh. "It's so like Ted to leave semi-cryptic notes on photos!"

Allison stared at her from above her mug. She joined in the laughter. "Yeah, I guess it is!"

Forty-Seven

Adia smoothed on red lipstick and pinned back her hair. *I'm to die for!* She turned in the mirror. *They're not going to know what hit them!* Grabbing the red woven bag from her closet, she went to the kitchen and slid the knife into its side pocket. *I'm probably gonna need a drink after this.* She opened her liquor cabinet and took out a silver flask and a fifth of Svedka. Adia took a swig and filled the flask. She spilled a few drops on the counter and blotted them up with a paper towel with one hand as she packed the flask away with the other. *Let's do this shit.* She opened the door and left.

It was almost dusk, and fireflies were darting in and out of the bushes surrounding Susan's porch. The clouds in the sky cast an orange haze on the neighborhood. Her red high heels click clacked as she ascended the porch steps. She knocked three times on the door. No one answered. *Where the fuck are they?* She clutched her bag to her side. *I'm glad I came prepared.* She sat down on the rocking chair and took out her flask. Watching a couple of kids ride by on their bicycles, she took a few sips. Adia tapped her fingers on the table and looked down the street. *No adults. Why the fuck are they not supervised? Don't their parents know that they could be abducted or killed?* She leaned back and took another sip. She rocked back and forth faster and faster. *Fuck this.* She stood up and walked to the corner liquor store. *I want more vodka.*

She returned with a handle of vodka and a jug of grape juice. Adia camped out on the porch again and chugged some grape juice to make room for the vodka. One drink turned into ten and she swayed to her feet and braced herself on the table. *If I'm going to do this, I'm going to do it big.* She took her fist and slammed it through the window. Groping through the glass, she unlocked the front door. With one push, the door opened and she stepped inside.

Then she heard it.

Beep.

Beep.

Two more shrill beeps came from somewhere. Adia dropped her bag on the floor. Her eyes widened as she wobbled to the sound's origin and tried to guess the password. *God damn it! I didn't think of this!* She punched the control device as a high-pitched shriek filled the house. Covering her ears, she half ran from the house before the authorities arrived. Her heel snapped and she fell against the warm concrete sidewalk.

Her head hit the ground with a soft smack. Adia pushed herself up to her feet. Her vision blurred even more as she attempted to run away. She made it ten feet before she felt her muscles tighten and then release. *Now, she'll definitely feel sorry.* She smiled. Night fell and she closed her eyes.

The boys sat on their bikes as the police arrived and watched as the officers searched the property. The blue and red contrasting with the descending darkness as the paramedics performed CPR on the unresponsive body.

Susan's car arrived as they were bagging Adia. She slowed down as an officer stopped her. Rolling down the window, she greeted the policewoman. "What's going on, officer? That's my house."

Allison sat in the passenger seat and clutched her pocketbook. She glanced from the house to the police to the paramedics to the bag to Susan and back to the house. An officer was exiting it. Something was in his hands. *What's that?* She squinted and caught the redness of Adia's bag.

She raised her eyebrows. *That's Adia's bag! I gave it to her for Christmas!* She turned her attention to Susan who was opening her door to answer some questions. The officer was jotting something down on her notepad.

Susan came to the open window. "Hey, baby, they need to ask you some questions."

Allison went numb as she unbuckled her seat belt and opened her door. *What's going on? Is Adia dead? Did she kill herself?* She ran her hand across the hood of the car as she made her way to the officer. She crossed her arms as she looked from the silver badge to her face.

The officer flipped a page in her notebook and started to write on a blank sheet. "Who are you?" she asked Allison.

"Allison Stanek." She tapped her fingers against her own arms.

"I'm Officer Martinez from the Omaha Police Department." She clicked her pen. "I need to ask you some questions."

"Ok." Allison watched another officer take Susan across the street.

"Do you know anyone who would try to harm your friend here?" Martinez pointed her pen toward Susan.

Is Susan going to be okay? Was Adia trying to kill her? "Yeah, my ex-girlfriend. Adia Dymek."

Martinez tapped her notepad. "Has Susan done anything recently that might have provoked Miss Dymek?"

Allison cocked her head. "No. We just started dating."

Martinez pointed toward Allison and then Susan. "You two?"

"Yeah." Allison rubbed the back of her ankle with her foot.

"I see." The officer pursed her lips together and wrote something down.

"What exactly is going on, Officer?" Allison glanced back at the paramedics who were closing their ambulance.

"We don't have all the details yet, but it looks like there was a break in."

The ambulance's engine started. "Who's in that ambulance?"

"We don't have an ID yet. Has Miss Dymek done anything rash, threatening lately?"

"Yeah. Last week, she attacked Susan." Allison looked at the notepad. "We filed a police report.

"I see."

"Then she confronted me in Target's parking lot a few days ago." Allison looked at the officer's holster. The streetlight shone on her gun.

"Tell me about that incident."

"Well, she blocked me in my parking spot

and apologized for attacking Susan. Adia got out of her car and tried to keep me from rolling my window up. She said that she treated me better than Susan." Allison let her arms down. "Then I shouted 'Get the hell away from me.' Then she left. That was it."

Officer Martinez clicked her pen again and put it in her pocket. "Thank you, Miss Stanek." She put her notepad in her back pocket. She then went over the male officer questioning Susan and compared notes. They nodded and switched places.

Allison pushed her hair behind her ears and answered the same questions. *I just want to go inside.* She glanced at the yellow police tape and the porch. *Is that glass?* A couple of investigators were taking pictures of the door. She could see the camera flashes inside the living room. *Was Adia trying to steal something?*

Susan came over and wrapped Allison in her arms. "Everything will be okay, Allie."

Allison felt her warm breath on her ear as she whispered. She turned her head toward her. "I hope so."

The two women stood there and watched the officers mill around the yard. Officer Martinez approached them. "Do you have any place you can stay until we finish with the crime scene?" she asked Susan.

Susan looked at Allison.

"She can stay at my apartment, Officer."

Martinez nodded. "Alright. May I have your phone number, Miss Johnson?"

"Yeah." Susan let go of Allison and wrote down her number on the officer's notepad.

"Thank you. We'll keep you updated." Martinez walked toward the other officers and put her hand on her hip.

Susan walked over to her car and opened the passenger side door. Allison paused between the door and the car and watched the blue and red lights flash against the house. "I wonder what really happened."

"I guess we'll find out soon enough." Susan closed the door. "You're really strong, Allie. I love that about you." She smiled. "You always manage to keep yourself together. I wish I could be like you."

Allison took her hand. "I'm not as strong as you."

Susan shook her head and drove down the dark street. A couple of raindrops hit the windshield. "Really, more rain?" Susan laughed as she hit the gas. "At least it's romantic, right?"

She's obviously ignoring it. She's silly like that. I want to help her realize her strength. Allison looked out the window and watched the neon lights fly past.

Forty-Eight

Susan stepped out on the porch the Wednesday after the funeral. The sun shone on the porch as she set her coffee on the table. The neighbor dragged his garbage cans to the side of the road. Remnants of police tape waved in the wind as cars passed and slowed down. *Everyone loves a good crime scene. What else is new?* Susan waved and they sped away. She heard the door creak as it opened and her lover stepped out with bed head and a cup of coffee in her hand. Allison sat down beside her and sipped her dark roast.

Two birds flew overhead into the clouds. "They say it's going to be a humid one today." Susan watched them fly in circles.

"I believe it." Allison leaned back. "We need a break from the rain."

"Oh, it'll probably rain again next week. Good Ol' Nebraska." Susan smiled and waved at a passing car.

"Probably. I wonder what will happen to this house?" Allison glanced at the porch ceiling.

"Ted's mom mentioned something along the lines of how I could stay here rent free until they figure out what to do with it." She waved again. "It'd be a shame for it to go to waste."

"Yeah. It's beautiful house underneath the chipped paint." Allison rubbed her hand against the wood. "And it has so much history."

"Yeah." Susan jolted. *I need to find what Ted left me.*

Allison looked at her phone. "I need to fix my hair before work." She stood up and took a few steps. "You coming in today?"

"Naw. I'm going to take a personal day." Susan took a long sip of coffee and set her cup down.

"Good, you need it, baby." Allison kissed her and went inside.

Susan followed and went into Ted's room. She moved the bed a few feet and felt along the floor. *There has to be a loose board here somewhere.* She spent a good five minutes testing out each board before she found the spot. Placing her hand on one end and applying some pressure, the other side lifted. She looked into the hole and found a wooden box. Taking it out, she examined it in both hands. It had to be cherry wood. She turned it around and found a name carved into the side. *Olivia Spencer.* Susan closed her eyes and braced herself before opening it. It gave a slight creak as she lifted the top. Inside was a piece of notebook paper and a bag. She unfolding the paper and read.

Dear Susan,

Here is a bag of the same type of coffee we enjoyed that day before we left for Omaha. I want you to savor it and think of me. Each time you drink it, remember me. I will always be with you through this as we are always part of this world. Emerson never died and neither did I. Remember that and be free. I love you.

Your brother,
Ted.

The door swung open and stiletto heels clacked across the tiles. Allison set a mug down in the sink as Sam approached the counter. *Allison always looks so cute. I wish I had her style.*

"Hey, Allison! What's up?" Sam took off her sunglasses and set her bag on the counter.

Allison shrugged. "Oh not much, just working, ya know?"

"Oh, sorry to interrupt." *Of course I fuck things up when I want to patch things up.*

"Eh, you're not really interrupting anything." Allison flicked her wrist toward the half-empty store. "We're pretty slow." She wiped her hands. "How are you?"

"I'm…I'm coping." *Well, as best I can anyway.* "Is Susan here?" She looked around.

"No, she took the day off." She leaned on the counter. "What's up?"

Susan fumbled in her bag for a piece of paper. *I guess it won't hurt to start with her.* "I have this." She stuck out her hand.

Allison took the paper and examined it. "Narcotics Anonymous?"

Sam shook as she crossed her arms. "Yeah. I went to a meeting last night." She dropped her arm to her side. "They gave an assignment to apologize to anyone that we've hurt." Sam shifted her weight from one foot to another. "I thought I'd start with Susan." *Best to get the hardest one out of the way.*

Allison set the paper down on the counter and slid it toward her. "You don't have to show me this." She clasped her hands together in front of her apron. "However, I plan on heading over to Susan's after work tonight, if you'd like to join me."

Why is she so nice? I have done nothing but hurt people. "S…Sure." Sam grabbed her bag.

"I'm off at five today." Allison smiled at a customer entering the shop. "Would you like to meet here?"

"Okay." Sam slid her bag onto her shoulder. Her stomach felt uneasy. *Why am I so nervous?*

It's just a goddamn apology. She turned to leave.

"Oh, and Sam."

Sam stopped. "Yeah?"

"I'm happy that you're doing well." Allison smiled again and Sam left the store.

Susan lay down on the couch and turned on her Internet radio. Sweet, slow acoustic music filled the living room and enveloped her in its ambient comfort. She let her mind lift and sway along as she fell into a gentle slumber that lasted a few moments but felt like years. Rubbing her eyes, she sat up and rose with effort to make her way to the kitchen for some more coffee. *What should I do today?* She stared through the kitchen window as she lifted the mug to her lips. *Ted, what would you do today?* Susan watched a cloud move across the sky. She smiled. *I knew it.*

She chugged her coffee and left the house. Opening her car door, she slammed it shut. *Shit! I forgot my wallet!* She ran inside and grabbed it from the kitchen table. In her haste, she knocked a stack of papers over, sending a flood of photos and debris over the table. She bent down to pick some up off the floor and turned one over, revealing a couple of college kids holding up beers and each other. Susan sat down and stared at the picture. She clasped her hand over her lips as a wave of silent tears ran down her face onto her lap. *We were sophomores thinking we were big shots.* She smiled and tasted a hint of salt. *We had so much fun that year!*

She wiped her tears away and stuck the picture in her wallet. *Ted, we always had so much fun, even when we slaved through our "study parties!" We never really studied during those, did we?* Susan filled a thermos with coffee. She laughed as she left and locked the house. Susan looked at the broken glass. *I really need to fix that.* She jiggled her keys in her hands. *I wonder how Allison feels now that Adia's gone. I bet she's relieved, but if I were her, I'd still be shaken up a bit. I should let her know just how awesome she is. But first I need to do this.*

She backed out of her driveway and drove out west, past the sub-districts and new shopping centers. She drove until she hit gravel. Pulling over, she closed her eyes. *I love you, Ted.* She exhaled and opened her car door to green wheat and far away cattle. Walking across the damp gravel, she felt the breeze rustle her hair. Her hand touched the aged, wooden fence in front of her. She set the thermos of coffee down in the grass and gauged the sturdiness of the post. Susan climbed on top of it and found her balance.

Remember that day, Ted? Right before we graduated? She stretched her hands up in the air and embraced the wind and sunshine. *I feel you, Ted. You're everywhere.* The sun warmed her face and she smiled.

After some time, she jumped down and picked up her thermos. She went back to her car and sat on the hood. Sipping her coffee, she watched two birds fly in the distance. She thought of that morning and Allison's dream. *Fucking weird ass coincidences.* She leaned back and closed her eyes. *Fucking weird ass life. It'll go on, though, just like everything else does. In a few years, I'll see you again. But not yet; I have things to do.* A bird crowed in the distance. *Yeah, I hear ya.* She put her hands behind her head and savored the damp smell of the earth. *I'll see you later.*

Five o'clock came around and Susan pulled into her driveway as Allison pulled up to the curb. She shut her car off and got out. *Who's that in the passenger seat? Is that...Is that...Sam? Why the fuck is she here? I don't want to fucking see her.*

"Sam?" She shielded her eyes from the sun.

"Hey, Susan, what's up?" Sam almost stumbled in the grass as she approached her.

"Not much. I just got back." Susan took a few steps toward the porch. "How are you?" *I don't know what to say to her. She wasn't at her own fucking boyfriend's funeral!*

"I'm…I'm coping." Sam followed her up the steps.

"Oh?" Susan cocked her eyebrow. "Is that why you weren't at the funeral?"

"No…I was there." She fussed with her purse.

"I didn't see you." *She must be lying.*

"I was in the very back." She almost tripped over her feet and trembled for a moment before sitting. "Truth is, I left and came back."

Is she okay? She's shaking. Is she even telling the truth? "Oh?" Susan unlocked the door and threw her wallet on the chair before coming outside. Allison came up and kissed her.

"Babe, I'm going to make some coffee. All three of us need to have some girl talk." She slipped past her and went to the kitchen.

Susan shut the door as Allison opened the cupboard and took out a bag of ground coffee.

"So, Sam." Susan sat down beside her. "What brings you here?" *I hope she doesn't leave more syringes around. That shit's dangerous.*

278

"I...I wanted to talk to you." Sam rubbed her hands against her arms. She rocked back and forth.

"I went to Narcotics Anonymous last night."

What? Susan sat and watched her behavior. She started to say something, but stopped as Sam started to say something.

"We were...g...given an a...assignment last night. W...we need to apologize to everyone we've hurt." Sam looked down and rubbed her feet together. "I...can't apologize to T...Ted, so I wanted to start with you." She started crying. "I...I know we've never really got along, but I want to start a friendship. I want to s...start over." She stopped and looked at Susan through her tears. "I want to be sober." She put her head in her hands.

Susan watched her with wide eyes. *Oh, my God. She's serious.* She got up and drew Sam into a tight hug. "I know, Sam, I know." Susan found herself crying into her shoulder. "I'm here for you. I want to help." She broke the embrace and held Sam at arm's length. "You are welcome here any time."

The door creaked open and more glass fell from the window as Allison came out with a carafe of hot coffee. She chuckled. "You gotta fix that window, Susan." She set three cups on the table and poured Sam's first. "This is nice, Sumatran coffee. It's full of earthy flavor."

Sam gave a slight smile. "Thank you, Allison." She spilled some as she shook.

Allison grabbed her hand. "You're welcome."

Sam looked from her to Susan and smiled. "I know." She trembled again. "I'm also leaving Omaha in a few months."

"Why?" Allison asked as she sipped some more coffee.

"I just need to escape. I need to find myself. I need to return to Denver." She looked down. "I know I can't quit cold turkey, but I think my friend Kyle would help me out." She traced a poor circle on the table. "He has a kid now, so that means he's got his shit together." She lifted her cup.

That's not how it works, but whatever. Susan watched her turquoise hair tumble with the wind. *At least you won't be here.*

The three women sat and talked about nothing and everything for hours. Susan smiled and watched her girlfriend and Sam laugh and carry on. *I guess I can tolerate Sam, even if I can't forgive her. This is life.* She leaned back and smiled.

Forty-Nine

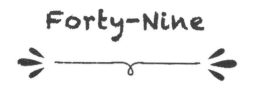

Allison waved Sam away as she dropped her off at her apartment. *I'm so glad they talked things out. Maybe Ted's death was a gift?* She shook her head. *No, nothing is gained in death. I hope Susan framed that picture I found. It's so profound.* Allison heard a can of spray paint fall in the back seat as she turned a corner. *I know what I should do right now.* Allison turned up the radio and hopped on the interstate. She cruised for an hour before she found a suitable billboard near Creighton hospital. She got off the interstate and parked a few blocks away in a back alley.

She slipped on her bandana and black hoodie. *Ugh, it's so humid.* She got the can of spray paint and shook it. *This should be enough.* She removed the safety and replaced the cap. Placing it in her front pocket, she climbed the rickety ladder. *I have to be quick.* She looked down. *I hope people appreciate the fact that I cheat death on a regular basis.* She continued climbing until she reached a somewhat sturdy scaffold. Allison lifted herself and began.

This piece only took half her usual time. She

looked up and smiled. *This is my best work thus far!* She climbed down and ran behind buildings and back to her car. Removing her disguise, she gunned it to the interstate. She watched her masterpiece disappear in her rear view mirror. She grinned and headed home.

She opened the front door and leaped into Susan's arms. "I love you!"

"I love you, too!" Susan matched her grin.

"I painted tonight!" Allison kissed her.

"Haha! What did you do this time?"

"You'll find out in the morning!" She pulled Susan into the bedroom.

"I can't wait!"

The next morning, all the media outlets were buzzing with the latest exploits of the ninja. School children stopped and smiled at the bus stop. College students stopped and stared on their way to class, resulting in several dropped books. Drivers slowed down. Everyone was smiling. Even the police had nothing negative to say.

Up in the clear sky, a billboard stood out. Red script was scrawled against its black and white background. It simply read, "Don't stop living. You are loved."

Acknowledgements

I want to thank everyone who helped me during my darkest days. You know who you are.

More Info:

If you or someone you love is considering self-harm, please reach out to one of these resources immediately:

The Suicide Hotline:
1.800.273.8255

The Trevor Project
1.866.488.7386

You are loved. Remember that.

About the Author:

Sarah Rowan graduated from Northwest Missouri State University in 2011 with a Bachelor's of Science in English Education. She has been writing since third grade. Her poetry has appeared in the *Girls Rule Boys Drool* zine, and *A Collection of Poetry by a Smartass Cynic*, *A Wannabe Albino*, and *A Cunning Linguist* (and many, many others). She released a self-published chapbook in 2012 titled *Doors*. *A Good Life* is her breakout novel. She aspires to write more and collect cats.

A Message From the Author:

Thank you for taking the time to read my book. I would be honored if you would consider leaving a review for it on *Amazon*.

Check out these books from
Amazing Things Press

Keeper of the Mountain by Nshan Erganian

Rare Blood Sect by Robert L. Justus

Survival In the Kitchen by Sharon Boyle

Stop Beating the Dead Horse by Julie L. Casey

In Daddy's Hands by Julie L. Casey

MariKay's Rainbow by Marilyn Weimer

Seeking the Green Flash by Lanny Daise

Thought Control by Robert L. Justus

Fun Activities to Help Little Ones Talk by Kathy Blair

Bighorn by James Ozenberger

Post Exodus by Robert Christiansen

Rawnie's Mirage by Marilyn Weimer

All American Prizefighter by Rob Calloway

Fall of Grace by Rachel Riley and Sharon Spiegel

Taming the Whirlwind by Lindsey Heidle

John Henry's War by Larry W. Anderson

The Brothers' Murder by Brenda Grant

Check out these Poetry books/Collections from
Amazing Things Press

Evoloving by James Fly

Starlings by Jeff Foster

Nightmares or Memories by Nona j. Moss

Tales From Beneath the Crypt by Megan Marie

Palightte by James Fly

Vintage Mysteries by Megan Marie

Tears and Prayers by Harold W. "Doc" Arnett

Thoughts of Mine by Thomas Kirschner

Inner Reflections by Shivonne Jean Hancock

Scanner Code by David Noe

Blanc Mange by Jeff Foster

Zenphoniquely by James Fly

Kin by David Noe

Voices in My Pen by David Noe

Thoughts of Mine II by Thomas Kirschner

Amazing Things Press

www.amazingthingspress.com